Preface

There was a time when every path felt like it led somewhere unknown.
A patch of woods became an unexplored wilderness. A creek became a river worth following. An old map, a hidden trail, or a strange object half-buried in the dirt could spark questions that lingered for days.

On summer afternoons, bicycles carried us farther than they should have. Tree forts became hidden outposts. Flashlights turned blankets into secret headquarters. The world felt larger then. Full of mysteries waiting to be uncovered and adventures waiting to begin.

Even on cold, rainy days when the weather kept us indoors, our imaginations refused to stay still. We searched old books for clues. Drew maps to places that did not yet exist. Dreamed of forgotten treasures, distant horizons, and worlds hidden just beyond sight.

But what if that feeling never truly left?
What if something is still waiting beyond the next hill, beneath the surface of the water, or hidden where few people think to look?
As we grow older, responsibilities multiply, schedules fill, and familiar places begin to feel smaller than they once did. Yet something inside us continues to stir whenever we hear a great story, uncover a mystery, or glimpse the possibility of something more.

The desire to explore.
To discover.
To become.

Frogman Puck was born from that feeling.

This is not simply a story about diving beneath the surface of the water. It is about friendship, courage, mystery, and the callings that quietly shape our lives. It is about hidden places, forgotten clues, impossible challenges, and the adventures that awaken something deeper within us.

Some adventures change where we go.
Others change who we become.
The greatest ones do both.

If you will come with us, set aside the noise of the world for a little while. Leave behind the deadlines, distractions, and demands waiting beyond these pages. Bring your sense of wonder. Bring your curiosity. Bring the part of you that still believes there may be more to discover.

There are mysteries in the deep.
Secrets beneath dusty sheets in forgotten places.
Clues hidden in plain sight.
Questions waiting for those willing to follow them.

Whether you are young, or simply remember what it felt like to be, there is a place for you here.

So take a deep breath.
The water is calm.
The mystery is waiting.

And somewhere beyond the shoreline, an adventure is about to begin.

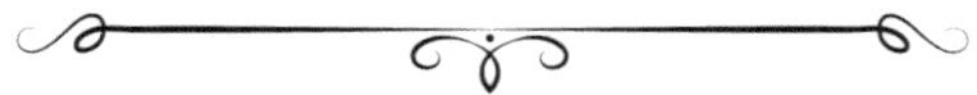

Frogman Puck Origins: The Rising Tides

The Legends Awaken: A Hero's Dream Quest

Illustrated Novel Edition

**Library of Congress Control Number:
2024926800**

About the Name 'Puck'

"Puck," "Puck-a-rino," and "Pitter-Puck" are affectionate nicknames bestowed by John Chanaca Sr. upon young dreamers and adventurers- those with boundless creativity, a thirst for exploration, and the courage to step into the unknown. These names, rooted in a cherished family tradition rather than folklore, serve as a call to embrace the spirit of youthful wonder and forge one's heroic journey.
As Scripture reminds us, "You intended to harm me, but God intended it for good to accomplish what is now being done, the saving of many lives" (Genesis 50:20). God has a way of transforming circumstances for His glory, and in this story, "Puck" represents the boundless joy, courage, and purpose found in a life guided by Him.

**Publisher: MJChanacapublishing LLC,
Family Values Series
ISBN-13: 978-1963416275 Paperback,
ISBN-13: 978-1963416282 Hardcover,
ISBN-13: 978-1963416268 EBOOK**

Welcome to Team TIDES

If you're reading this, you've just stepped into the world of Frogman Puck, and I'm genuinely glad you're here.

Whether someone shared this adventure with you or simply stumbled across it while searching for your next great read, welcome.

This book was written for readers who still believe there's something magical about discovery. The kind of readers who remember wondering what might be hidden beneath the surface, where forgotten clues might lead, and how one ordinary adventure can change a life forever.

I hope these pages remind you of that feeling.

This isn't just the beginning of Puck's journey.

It's the beginning of ours.

Team TIDES is more than the characters you'll meet in this story. It's a growing community of readers who love mystery, adventure, imagination, and stories that remind us courage, friendship, faith, and character still matter.

Over the coming months, you'll receive behind-the-scenes artwork, early looks at new books, exclusive illustrations, special updates, and opportunities to become part of future launches. I think you'll enjoy seeing how this world continues to grow.

For now, I ask only one thing.

Enjoy the adventure.

If this story makes you smile, sparks your imagination, or reminds you of the wonder you felt growing up, then you've already given me the greatest gift an author could receive.

When you reach the final page, if you'd like to help Team TIDES continue growing, I'd be grateful if you shared your thoughts with other readers by leaving an honest review on Amazon, Goodreads, BookBub, or your favorite reading platform. Every review helps another adventurer discover this world.

Now...

Take a deep breath.

The water is calm.

The mystery is waiting.

And somewhere beyond the shoreline...

your adventure begins.

—Joel Chanaca

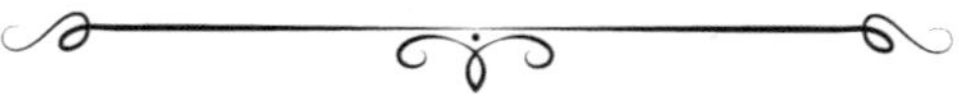

Chapters

Tides of Imagination

Cold raindrops raced down the windowpane as young Puck, his eyes wide with wonder, dove into another underwater adventure book. Outdoor play was out of the question on this dreary day. The Outdoor Channel and these vibrant pages became his portal to aquatic realms. His living room transformed into an underwater observation deck, the rain-streaked windows morphing into portholes to a watery world.

Vivid fish seemed to dart between the fibers of the rug, while outside his window, a giant sea turtle gazed at him, its ancient eyes full of secrets from the deep. Puck often wondered what it would be like to swim into the ocean's depths, exploring the hidden world beneath the surface. He knew he couldn't breathe underwater like a fish or hold his breath for very long like a turtle or a frog. He had tried, watching the clock tick on the wall, but it was never long enough to explore as much as he wanted. Still, this limitation only fueled his determination to find a way to unlock the mysteries of the underwater world.

As Puck sat on the couch, book in hand, he felt a stirring in his heart-a calling that whispered of grand adventures and incredible discoveries waiting just beyond the shore. Little did he know that his childhood fascination was the first ripple in a wave that would carry him toward an extraordinary destiny. With each page he turned or show he watched, Puck was unknowingly preparing himself for a future filled with excitement and the fulfillment of his wildest dreams. The water was calling to him, and one day, he would answer, diving headfirst into a world of wonder that would change his life forever.

THE OCEAN
EXPLORATION & DISCOVERY
THE DEEP
OCEAN WONDERS
JOURNEYS BELOW

It wasn't just the sea creatures that captivated Puck. What truly held his attention were the mysterious people exploring the world beneath the waves. Clad in sleek suits and equipped with fascinating gear, they moved through the water with grace and purpose.

Puck watched in awe as streams of silvery bubbles trailed behind these underwater adventurers, rising in spiraling columns to the surface. He imagined the bubbles as secret messages, carrying whispers of hidden treasures and untold stories from the depths below.

These explorers seemed to possess a unique ability to breathe underwater, defying the limitations of land dwellers. Their masks and tanks resembled something out of a science fiction story, allowing them to venture deeper and stay longer in the mysterious realm that so vividly captivated the young boy.

Puck didn't know who these underwater adventurers were, but in his mind, he began to call them Bubble-Up Men. He marveled at their bravery as they ventured into the unknown depths where sunlight barely reached.

As he watched them glide effortlessly through schools of colorful fish and past swaying coral reefs, Puck felt a stirring in his heart. One day, he promised himself, he would join their ranks. One day, he too would explore the hidden wonders of the deep, leaving a trail of bubbles in his wake.

As Puck grew, so did his love for underwater adventures. At night, he dreamed of the underwater world, imagining bubbles rising and popping at the surface. He could see all types of colorful fish and the daylight shining through the water.

Puck sensed the water gently moving around him and heard what the aquatic realm might sound like. His dreams were filled with mystery and adventure.

The Dreams of Starlight Cove

One evening, Puck and his neighbor, Tad, visited a place between their houses in the woods, Starlight Cove. This was their secret spot, where the water was mostly shallow and shimmered like stars. It was close to home, and their parents had given them one simple rule: stay away from the deep end.

After skipping stones, Puck asked Tad, "Have you ever seen the 'Bubble-up Men' on TV?"

Tad chuckled. "Bubble-up Men? What do you mean?"

"They dive deep into the ocean," Puck explained, his face lighting up. "They wear fins, masks, and big air tanks. When they breathe, bubbles float to the surface like tiny silver balloons!"

Tad laughed. "Ah, frogmen-or SCUBA divers. They explore the underwater world," said Tad.

"Frogmen? How cool is that? I want to be a frogman one day," said Puck.

Puck began practicing swimming and snorkeling at the local high school pool, working hard to build his skills. As he grew more confident, he advanced to training in ponds and lakes at nearby state park recreational areas, where experienced lifeguard trainers helped him become a junior lifeguard. Each new challenge fueled his excitement.

The idea of becoming a frogman consumed Puck's imagination. He spent hours sketching scenes of divers exploring coral reefs, shipwrecks, and mysterious sea creatures. In his mind, he could see bubbles swirling in the water, sunlight streaming down in beams, and the endless blue waiting to be discovered. With every stroke of his pen, the underwater world felt closer.

One Saturday morning, Puck's parents surprised him with a brand-new fish tank. The moment he laid eyes on the colorful fish gliding through the water, he was mesmerized. Hours would pass as he watched them dart between the plants, imagining himself swimming alongside them. Each fish had a name, and he studied their movements with fascination.
One morning, Puck became so lost in watching his fish that he didn't hear the clock ticking. The sound of his mother's voice snapped him out of his trance.
"Puck, you missed the bus!" she said urgently.
Puck's stomach dropped. "Mom, can you call Grandma for me while I get ready?" he pleaded, hoping for a reprieve.
"No, Puck. You need to take responsibility," his mom replied. "You'll have to call Grandma yourself and remember to pay her for gas from your chore allowance. She might not want to accept it, so leave the money on the seat when you get out. I can't stay; I'll be late for work."

Reluctantly, Puck made the call and arranged for the ride. When they arrived at school, he slipped the money onto the car seat, feeling the sting of using his hard-earned allowance.

Later that evening, Puck's mother sat down beside him. "It's wonderful that you love your fish, but you need to find a balance so that you don't miss other important things," she said gently.

Puck nodded, understanding the lesson. From that day forward, he made sure to take care of his responsibilities first, watching his fish only after everything was done. It was a small shift, but it taught him that passion and responsibility could swim side by side.

School
Math Test
Book Report
Vocabulary
History
Field Trip
8:17
SEA TURTLES
A COMPLETE GUIDE
WHALES
UNDERWATER PHOTOGRAPHY

Puck and Tad had a tradition. Every weekend, after finishing their chores, they would head to Starlight Cove to explore and talk about the underwater world. As they gazed out over the still waters, Tad would share stories of daring missions, deep-sea adventures, and the mysteries hidden beneath the ocean's surface.

"One day, we'll be down there," Puck said, "exploring like real frogmen." They spent hours imagining themselves suited up in sleek dive gear, breathing through their tanks, and uncovering hidden treasures. Their dream was as vibrant as the friendship they shared.

On the boy's next visit, the air at Starlight Cove felt different. Tad was quieter than usual, his eyes lingering on the horizon. Finally, he broke the silence.
"Puck, I have some bad news." His voice was steady, but there was a sadness in it.
Puck turned, his heart sinking before he even heard the words.
"My dad got a job in another town. We're moving!"

The weight of Tad's words hung in the air. For a moment, neither of them spoke. Starlight Cove suddenly felt too quiet for the first time.

"When?" Puck managed to ask, though he already knew the answer.
"Soon. But no matter what happens, we'll always share this dream, right? We'll still become frogmen," Tad replied with determination.
Puck nodded, forcing a smile. "Always."
Tad added, "Puck, I know you listen to your parents, get things done, and you're a big dreamer. You also need to know that dreams don't just come true by chance. You have to balance yourself, set goals, and follow through. If you get knocked down, you've got to get right back up and try again. Can you do that?"

Puck quickly replied, "If that's what it takes to get me to our dream, you bet I can!"
They sat together in silence a little longer, watching the cove that had been theirs for so long. It was a place of dreams, and despite the coming change, their shared dream would live on-even if Tad wasn't right by his side.

Puck missed Tad after he moved away, but they stayed in touch, sharing stories of their adventures. As time passed, Puck found new ways to keep busy. He helped his mom around the house and often reminisced about the fun he and Tad had at Starlight Cove.

One day, Puck told his mother, "We're still going to be frogmen, Mom. We'll explore all the underwater worlds. Tad said that if we balance our time and set goals, we can make our dream come true."

His mother smiled. "That's great advice. I've always liked Tad, and I'm sorry he had to move, but I've appreciated the extra help around the house. Your dad and I have noticed how motivated you are, and we've decided to give you an allowance for the extra chores. That way, you can start saving for your training."

Puck grinned. "Thanks, Mom! I'll save every penny. I'm one step closer to becoming a frogman!"

Where the Water Meets the Air

Once his chores were done, Puck had time to explore his favorite interests. He read books about the ocean, sketched pictures of underwater worlds, and kept dreaming of becoming a frogman. Even without Tad, Starlight Cove was still his special place, where his dreams could grow.

One afternoon, while Puck was sitting by the water, lost in thought, he realized he wasn't alone. A boy about his age had wandered over from the path through the woods, Tad's old path.

Puck smiled. "Hey, I'm Puck. How's it going?"

The boy kicked at the ground, shrugged, and sat down. "I'm Zane. I guess I'm fine. This place is all right, but it's nothing compared to our old house near the airfield. Soon, I'll be busy taking classes to get my pilot's license."

Puck's eyes widened. "You're going to be a pilot? That's awesome!"

Zane smirked. "Yeah, flying's a real adventure, you know? It's a lot more exciting than splashing around in the water like a fish."

Puck felt a twinge of frustration. "Well, being a frogman is an adventure too. Exploring deep underwater, discovering new things, it's not as easy as it sounds."

Zane shrugged again and plopped down on a rock. "Maybe, but I'm sticking with the skies. The water doesn't seem that interesting to me."

For the first time, Puck felt a little unsure. Maybe his dream wasn't as exciting as he'd always thought.

All week, Puck was troubled by what Zane had said. So, after finishing his chores, he went to Starlight Cove for a moment of peace, only to see Zane strolling down the path.
"Hey, Zane!" Puck called out, trying to ignore his frustration.

Zane slouched over, kicking at the rocks as he walked. "Hey," he muttered, hopping onto a large rock barely poking out of the water.
Puck tilted his head, sensing something was wrong. "What's up?"

Zane huffed. "I was at the airfield yesterday, you know, trying to get a closer look at the planes. But this older teen who works there gave me a hard time. Said I was in the way. He's always like that-thinks he knows everything just because he works there."
Puck listened, nodding. "That stinks. People like that can get to you."
Zane sighed. "Yeah, I can't wait to fly. I won't have to deal with guys like him anymore. Anyway, I don't understand why you hang around this cove so much. It seems kind of boring to me," he said as he jumped to a rock on the deep side of the cove.
Puck smiled, pointing toward the deeper water. "There's more than you think. It's pretty dangerous over there if you're not careful."

Zane waved him off. "Pfft, I'm not scared of a little water."
Puck's expression tightened. "Seriously, Zane, you shouldn't-"
Before Puck could finish, Zane lost his balance and slipped into the deeper end of the cove, disappearing beneath the surface.

Without hesitation, Puck jumped into the water. He swam down quickly, grabbed Zane's arm, and pulled him to safety. Coughing and sputtering, Zane sat up on the shore, his face pale with shock.

After catching his breath, Puck said, "I told you that part is dangerous! Are you okay?"

Zane nodded, embarrassed but grateful. "Yeah, thanks... I didn't realize it was that deep."

They sat quietly for a moment before Zane muttered, "Guess I've had two bad days in a row."

Puck chuckled. "Hey, we all have rough days. But look-whether it's flying or diving, we both want to do something big and exciting! We're going to hit bumps along the way."

Zane looked at him. "Yeah... maybe. That guy at the airfield got to me, though."

Puck leaned back, staring at the sky. "You know, I've had doubts too. But we can't let people like that stop us. We can work through it and help each other when we can."

Zane nodded slowly, starting to feel a connection. "Maybe you're right. Sorry, I've poked fun at your love for the water. I was frustrated about the move and shouldn't have taken it out on you."

Puck smiled. "I get it. Zane, you're all right by me!"

From that day on, Puck and Zane began finding ways to help each other-whether it was Puck sharing tips around the water or Zane talking about overcoming nerves at the airfield. They had different goals, but they realized they weren't so different after all.

Echoes from Below

One Sunday after church, while visiting his grandparents, something unexpected caught Puck's attention. As he played in the front yard, the door of the neighbor's shed creaked open, and his eyes widened in awe. Inside, shelves were packed with mysterious frogman gear, masks, fins, air tanks, and more. Then, to Puck's astonishment, Mr. Becker stepped out, clad in a brand-new frogman suit.

Mr. Becker waved and called out, “Hey, Puck! Why don’t you ask your family if you can come check out my new gear? I remember them telling me that you’re interested in scuba diving!”

Buzzing with excitement, Puck raced inside. “Can I go see Mr. Becker’s gear?” he asked eagerly.
His grandfather chuckled. “You sure can, Puck-a-rino!”
Hearing the commotion, Puck’s dad chimed in, “I’ll come too!”

Without hesitation, Puck and his dad hurried back across the yard. Mr. Becker greeted them and dove into an explanation of how each piece of gear worked, from the hefty air tanks to the sleek, streamlined fins. As he talked, Puck's eyes were drawn to the array of frogman equipment in different sizes and colors, each more advanced than the last.
With a glint in his eye, Mr. Becker handed Puck some top-of-the-line gear to try out. “Go ahead,” he said with a nod. “Give it a try.”

Puck slipped on the mask and took a deep breath, the cool air rushing in as he imagined a daring underwater rescue deep inside a flooded submarine. It felt hyper-realistic, as if he were there, his senses connected to everything around him.
“One day, I’ll teach you how to dive for real, Puck,” Mr. Becker said.
Puck’s heart surged with excitement, his dreams edging closer to reality.

As Puck grew older, his dream of becoming a frogman remained strong. He knew that dreams didn't come true on their own-they required hard work and focus.
Puck made a plan. He carefully balanced his time between swimming laps to build strength, studying hard in school, and helping his family.

He made new friends at school and while volunteering with his church in the community. Every night before bed, he marked another day off his calendar, knowing it brought him one step closer to his dream.
He felt happy with his progress and often visited Starlight Cove with Zane. Zane had figured out how to handle the older teen at the airfield by offering to help with his work duties. To Zane's surprise, this opened new doors, giving him more opportunities to learn about planes. Though their dreams pointed in different directions-Puck toward the deep underwater world and Zane toward the skies-they discovered they shared a common foundation. Both boys realized that having a strong foothold on the ground and in life would help them reach the depths or heights of their dreams.

From time to time, Puck and Tad would catch up on both old and new times. Tad remained committed to becoming a frogman and had signed up for junior diving classes in his new town. Puck was happy for Tad's opportunity and was grateful to learn from the extra insights Tad shared with him after classes started.

The Bottle in the Attic

Mr. Matt's shop, nestled along the banks of the Old Blackwater River, was a treasure trove of local history and adventure gear. From safety equipment to kayaks ready for river excursions, the store had it all. But what truly captured Puck's imagination was a secluded corner displaying old glass bottles, curious shark teeth, ancient maps, and Native American artifacts that whispered tales of the river's rich past.

One fateful day, Mr. Matt, his eyes twinkling with excitement, beckoned Puck to follow him up a creaky, winding staircase to the shop's attic. The musty air was thick with the scent of aged wood and forgotten memories. Dust motes danced in the thin shafts of light that pierced through the small, grimy windows.

"There's something special up here, Puck," Mr. Matt said, his voice hushed with reverence. "Some of my grandfather's old stuff. Do you mind going through it and seeing if you can clean it up a bit? Something up here might look good in the shop."

In a far corner, beneath a tattered sheet, stood an old sea chest. With curiosity, Puck lifted the lid, revealing a collection of bottles, each more intriguing than the last. But one stood out. It was an ornate, emerald-green bottle with strange symbols etched into its surface. The bottle also bore a unique octopus symbol, its tentacles swirling in an intricate design, as if hiding a deeper meaning.

As Puck carefully lifted it from the chest and set it down on another old trunk, a chill ran down his spine. The bottle felt heavier than it should, as if weighted with secrets. Mr. Matt's eyes widened, a mix of awe and apprehension flashing across his face.

"My grandfather spoke of this bottle," Mr. Matt whispered, running his fingers over the glass surface. "He always said it held clues to something important, but he could never figure out how to reveal its secrets. I remember him mentioning a riddle, a sort of key. Let me see... it went like this:

'Eyes may see but not perceive,
What lies within, few could conceive.
With light's embrace, the truth appears,
To guide the lost, when all becomes clear.'

"Yeah, that's it. But what do you think it means?"
Puck stared at the bottle, deep in thought. "The first part-'Eyes may see but not perceive,' could mean that even though we're looking right at it, there's more to this bottle than we realize. Like... we're seeing it, but we're not truly understanding what's inside. Maybe it's hidden in plain sight. And 'what lies within, few could conceive'-maybe the secret is something so incredible, most people wouldn't even believe it if they saw it."

"That makes sense," Mr. Matt said thoughtfully. "What about the rest?"
"The bottle is made of glass, right?" Puck continued, leaning closer. "Glasses help people see clearly. So maybe the glass itself is important; it's what helps us perceive what we're missing. 'With light's embrace, the truth appears.' Maybe we need to reveal the secret inside. Light guides people in the dark... like how we can only see clearly when the stars or the moon are out at night."

Mr. Matt nodded slowly, still gazing at the bottle. "So, maybe we're looking at the right thing but in the wrong way. Something's missing."

Puck shrugged. "I don't know if we've figured it all out yet, but it feels like the answer is staring us right in the face. We just don't see it."

Back in the shop, Mr. Matt placed the bottle on his desk, his brow furrowed in thought. Puck couldn't shake the feeling that this bottle was more than just a relic. As he cleaned and organized the shop, he studied the other items, glancing at the bottle now and then. The riddle echoed in his mind. Each artifact seemed to hold a piece of the river's history, but this bottle... it felt like the beginning of a new chapter, one waiting to be written.

Later that evening, after sundown, Puck brought some final paperwork into Mr. Matt's office and set it on the desk. Mr. Matt sat in an armchair by the window overlooking the water. Hearing Puck enter, he turned to greet him, but as he swung the chair around, his elbow bumped the lamp and the emerald bottle, knocking them both over.

Mr. Matt moved quickly to catch the lamp, which teetered on the edge of the desk, while Puck grabbed the bottle just before it rolled off. As he held it, the light from the lamp shone through the glass, casting a soft, glowing green hue across the room. They both paused, marveling at the beautiful light.

"Will you look at that!" Mr. Matt exclaimed, his eyes wide with amazement.

Puck's gaze shifted to the wall, where the light filtered through the bottle's glass, casting the faint outline of a map.

"That's it!" he said, breathless. "That's the map-the answer to the riddle! But... what is it trying to show us?"

Mr. Matt moved the bottle and adjusted another lamp to sharpen the image on the back wall. "I'm not sure yet," he said, "but I know someone who might. We'll need to figure this out, one way or another."

A Deep Frogman Lesson

One day, while Puck was visiting his grandparents, they said, "Puck, you should head over to Mr. Becker's place. He wants to give you something and have a chat."

Puck raced across the yard, his heart pounding with excitement. He eagerly knocked on Mr. Becker's door.

Mr. Becker opened it with a warm smile. "Puck, glad you could make it. I've been looking forward to seeing you. There's something I want to show you in the garage. Come on."

Puck's mind buzzed with curiosity as he followed Mr. Becker, wondering what the surprise could be.

Mr. Becker continued, "Your grandparents have been telling me about the progress you're making with your swimming lessons. They're proud of how good you've become in the water. I also heard about you helping that boy who fell into the cove. And you've been doing great work over at Mr. Matt's shop. You know he's a good friend of mine, right?"

Puck's eyes widened. "You and Mr. Matt are friends?"

Mr. Becker chuckled. "Yes, for many years. Our families go way back. In fact, I've been digging into our shared history lately, learning more about where we came from and what's ahead. I have a few things for you. First, this."

He handed Puck several dive suits, masks, snorkels, and fins. "I think you're ready for the next step in your training. Those frog fins should fit perfectly. I have plenty, and you're welcome to any of this gear. Just report back how well it works for you."

Puck could hardly believe it. He ran his hands over the gear, feeling the weight of his growing responsibility. "Wow, thank you!"

Mr. Becker smiled, then handed him a book. "And this is a dive manual. It's time for you to start studying the science behind diving-things like math, physics, and water safety. These aren't just hobbies, Puck. You need to prepare physically and mentally when you're passionate about something. A deep understanding can help you improve as a diver or as a person of character."

Puck looked up, determination in his eyes. "I'll study hard. I want to be the best."

Mr. Becker nodded approvingly. "I know you will. Your name comes up often in town these days-and for good reasons."

Puck was surprised. "People like Mr. Matt?"

"Yes, and others," Mr. Becker said with a chuckle. "People notice when someone is putting in effort. Your work and attitude have already set a good example. But remember, balance is key."

Puck tilted his head, sensing something deeper in Mr. Becker's words. "Balance?"

Mr. Becker's tone softened. "A job well done is important, but so is making sure your life stays in check between work and play."

He paused, his eyes glinting with a knowing look. "Stay in the light, and you will see the path ahead."

He was referring to more than just diving; there was a hidden meaning connected to the emerald bottle Puck had discovered with Mr. Matt.

After a reflective moment, Mr. Becker brightened. "How about a quick bite before we clean up your new mask? A little toothpaste will do the trick, and then we'll head up to the high school pool to test your gear. I'll teach you a trick. How to spit in your mask to keep it from fogging up."

Puck's face lit up. "Spit in it? I thought I knew everything about diving, but that's new!"

Mr. Becker laughed. "And that's your next lesson: none of us know everything. We all have more to learn, and sometimes we need each other to grow."

A Trustworthy Diver

After eating some sandwiches, Mr. Becker and Puck cleaned Puck's new mask.

"All right, Puck, that's all set. How about we head over to the high school pool and test out your new gear?"

Puck's face lit up. "I can't wait! Let's go!"

But Mr. Becker raised a hand, a gentle reminder in his tone. "Before we do, your family knows I offered to take you, but you still need to check in with them first. You should always let your parents know where you'll be, especially when it comes to diving or any activity that takes you outside your usual routine. It's a good habit to have."

Puck nodded, understanding the seriousness in Mr. Becker's words. "Got it. I'll head back and make sure it's okay."

"Perfect. I'll load up the truck and wait for you in the driveway," said Mr. Becker.

With excitement buzzing in his chest, Puck dashed back to his grandparents' house, eager to show off his new gear and get permission for the pool trip. As he burst through the door, his family smiled at the sight of him with his new mask and fins.

"Look at you!" his grandmother exclaimed. "You're ready for the deep end, aren't you?"

Puck grinned from ear to ear. "Mr. Becker wants to take me to the high school pool to test out the gear. Is that all right?"

His dad chuckled, giving a nod of approval. "Of course. Just be careful and listen to Mr. Becker."

His grandmother added, "No wonder they call it frogman gear. Those fins look like frog feet. That's neat, Puck. We'd love to see you in action, but for now, we want you to have your special moment and put all your focus on Mr. Becker's instruction."

As Puck was about to turn and leave, his mother added, "Puck, I've got some good news. Tad is coming to spend the weekend with you! He's bringing his snorkeling gear. Would you like to use your gear at Starlight Cove?"

Puck's eyes widened in surprise. "Yes! Tad's coming? That's awesome!"

"Yes, his family is bringing him later this evening," his mother said.

Puck nodded enthusiastically. "Gear, training, and Tad are coming over. What a day! Thank you! I'll be back before you know it," he replied.

With his family's permission granted, Puck raced back to Mr. Becker's driveway, nearly tripping over his fins in his excitement.

"All set?" Mr. Becker asked as Puck reappeared, a grin plastered on his face.

"Yep! And guess what? Tad's coming to spend the weekend! We're going to snorkel together at Starlight Cove."

Mr. Becker smiled, pleased by the news. "Sounds like a perfect weekend. But first things first. Let's make sure you're comfortable with your gear in the pool. You need to practice in a safe environment before tackling the cove."

They arrived at the high school pool, where the water shimmered under the bright lights. Mr. Becker helped Puck adjust his fins and mask, explaining how to clear water from the snorkel and prevent the mask from fogging.

"Forget fancy antifog solutions. Just spit, smear, rinse, and you're good to go," Mr. Becker said. Then he added, "And remember, when you're coming up for air, look up at the surface and blow out as you break through. It takes less effort, and you won't end up spouting water like a whale on the other swimmers!"

Puck listened intently, his nerves giving way to focus. He wanted to be ready for the cove with Tad and knew this lesson was important.

After some time in the pool practicing dives and controlling his breath, Puck surfaced and pulled off his mask.

"This is amazing, Mr. Becker! I can't wait to show Tad what I've learned."

Mr. Becker nodded approvingly. "You're getting the hang of it. Just remember, check your gear, stay calm, and trust your training when you're out there with Tad. You're becoming a strong diver, Puck, but always respect the water."

Still catching his breath, Puck nodded and said, "Yes, sir. I will always respect it."

"Water can sustain life and take it away. Remember, you shouldn't treat it like you have control over it. Instead, learn to work with it, respect it, and appreciate it. Now that you're comfortable with the gear, it's time to take a lap with each piece individually. First, swim with just the mask, then only the fins. Finally, we'll fill your mask with water, and you'll swim calmly, focusing on breathing through the snorkel as it is held upright by the mask strap."

Puck replied, "I get it. You want me to be ready if something unexpected happens, right?"

"Exactly, Puck. You're on the right track."

As the lesson wrapped up, Puck dried off and thanked Mr. Becker for his guidance.

"I'll be ready for the cove now."

"You will be," Mr. Becker agreed with a smile. "But remember, you're always learning. Diving isn't just about being in the water; it's also about knowing when to push forward and when to hold back. Here, take these two new frogskin suits for you and Tad."

Puck nodded thoughtfully, feeling more prepared and responsible than ever before. He returned home with his parents, eagerly awaiting Tad's arrival. This weekend promised to be unforgettable...an adventure with his best friend at Starlight Cove and the start of something much deeper in his journey as a Frogman.

The Reunion in Starlight Cove

Later that evening, Tad's family arrived and shared a warm dinner with Puck's family before heading out for their weekend trip. After dinner, Puck and Tad took the chance to catch up on their latest adventures, discussing how their diving skills had progressed. Excitement buzzed between them as they talked about their plans for Starlight Cove the next morning. Before long, they turned in for the night, eager to be well-rested for the day ahead.

The next morning, after a hearty breakfast, both boys pitched in to help clean up. Then they checked in with Puck's parents, hoping for the all-clear to head to the cove.

"Can we go now?" Puck asked.

His mom smiled. "Yes, but your dad and I want to come with you-for safety. We trust you both, and we know you're ready, but we want everything to go smoothly."

Puck and Tad exchanged glances, nodding in understanding. They appreciated the support, even as they took this next step toward independence.

They all made their way to Starlight Cove. The sun sparkled off the water, and the boys eagerly suited up, ready to explore the deep end for the first time.

As they prepared to enter the water, Puck mentioned, "It's too bad Zane couldn't meet you this weekend, Tad. His family took him to an air show at the air base."

Tad shrugged, adjusting his mask. "Maybe next time."

Once in the water, Puck's parents watched proudly from the shore as the boys dove down and explored the depths of the cove, testing their skills and different equipment. They were enjoying the thrill of a new adventure.

It was a milestone moment-something they would remember for a long time. It was their first real taste of growing up, but with the steady support of family by their side.

Bridging Together: The Black Water Cleanup

The next morning, Puck got a call from Zane, who sounded as eager as ever.

"Hey, man! I'm home from the airshow. We were supposed to stay an extra day, but my parents asked if I wanted to come home early since Tad's visiting you this weekend. I couldn't pass that up."

Puck grinned, already buzzing with excitement. "That's awesome! Let's meet up at the marina. I've got an idea I want to run by you guys."

Within the hour, Puck, Zane, and Tad were strolling down the familiar path to Mr. Matt's shop by the marina. Tad was excited to hang out with both of them, especially after hearing so much about Zane. As they reached the docks, the cool breeze from the Old Blackwater River swept over them, carrying the scent of water and old boats. The marina was bustling with people fixing up their vessels and fishermen preparing for a day on the water.

The boys found a quiet spot near the shop to chat about Puck's new idea. Puck leaned forward, his enthusiasm contagious.

"So, I've been thinking... how cool would it be to organize a river clean-up? The Old Blackwater could use some help, and it'd be a way for us to give back."

Zane's eyes lit up. "That's perfect! I saw a lot of trash and old debris in the river near the docks the last time I was out. People would get behind this."

Tad nodded thoughtfully. "We've talked about making a difference for years, and this could be our first big step."

As they started brainstorming, another boy leaned against a boat nearby. They didn't notice him at first, but he was around their age and had been listening closely to everything they were saying. After a while, the boy walked off, heading toward the marina office with a determined look.

Tad spotted him out of the corner of his eye and frowned. "Hey, did you guys see that? That kid was totally listening to us. You think he's gonna try to run with our idea?"

Zane raised an eyebrow. "You think so? He seemed kind of shifty when he walked off."

Puck felt his stomach tighten. He didn't like the idea of someone stealing their plan, especially after they had just come up with it. But before he could let the anger simmer, something clicked. What if the boy wasn't trying to take their idea but instead was interested in helping? Jumping to conclusions wouldn't solve anything.

"Hold on," Puck said, holding up a hand. "Let's not get ahead of ourselves. We don't know for sure that he's doing anything wrong. What if he's just curious or even wants to help?"

Tad and Zane exchanged glances, still skeptical, but they trusted Puck's judgment.

Puck smiled slightly. "Let's go talk to him. If he's interested, we could use the extra help. This cleanup could be bigger than just the three of us."

The boys made their way over to the marina office, where the boy was chatting with one of the workers. When he noticed them approaching, he stiffened, clearly uneasy.

"Hey," Puck called out in a friendly tone. "We saw you hanging around, and we were talking about organizing a river cleanup. Would you be interested in helping us plan it?"

The boy looked surprised but quickly nodded. "Uh, yeah. I didn't mean to eavesdrop... It just sounded like a cool idea, and I didn't know how to ask."

Puck smiled, his earlier frustration melting away. "No worries. We're trying to make this a team effort. What's your name?"

"Wes. I'm visiting my grandparents," the boy said, looking relieved.

"Well, Wes," Puck continued, "we could use your help. We're still figuring out the logistics, but we want this to be a big event. The more hands on deck, the better."

Wes grinned, clearly excited to be part of something bigger. "I'm in."

The boys sat down at the marina picnic tables, pulling out their phones and starting to research which companies they could invite to support their clean-up effort. Zane quickly found an organization called Wounded Nature–Working Veterans, which specialized in removing large debris from waterways and abandoned boats.

"Check this out," Zane said, showing the others his phone. "These guys are pros at this kind of thing. Rudy and Whit could help us out."

Tad jumped in next. "Green Environmental could bring dumpsters. They're known for supporting local community events."

"And we could ask the Solid Waste Authority at the landfill to waive the dump fees," Puck added. "That way, it won't cost the community anything."

"Wait-what about getting some muscle?" Wes chimed in. "I know there's a guy named Arron who runs a dumpster company. He could bring extra dumpsters."

Puck added, "And maybe we could even get Brox with his barge and trackhoe to help pull out the heavy stuff, like old docks and abandoned boats."

Tad's eyes widened. "That's brilliant. With all these people involved, this could be huge."

The boys spent the rest of the afternoon contacting each organization. To their surprise, everyone they reached out to was eager to get involved. Rudy and Whit from Wounded Nature agreed to bring a team, Green Environmental offered dumpsters, and the Solid Waste Authority confirmed they would waive the fees. Arron and Brox volunteered their equipment; they were both excited to help clean up the river they loved.

On the day of the event, dozens of people showed up to help. Rudy and Whit, along with Brox and Ryan, the trackhoe operator, extracted large debris and vessels. The dumpsters filled quickly, but Green Environmental and Arron were ready with backups, ensuring everything was hauled off efficiently. Puck, Zane, Tad, and Wes worked side by side with the professionals, coordinating efforts and keeping the volunteers motivated. As the hours passed, the Old Blackwater River began to look cleaner than it had in years. The boys couldn't believe the transformation happening right before their eyes. At one point, Puck stopped to take it all in. It wasn't just about cleaning up the river anymore-this was about showing what people could accomplish when they worked together for a common cause.

"I can't believe we pulled this off," Tad said, wiping sweat from his forehead. "This is bigger than I ever imagined."

Zane grinned. "Yeah, and it's only the beginning. There's so much more we can do."

Puck nodded. He looked at his friends, Zane, Tad, and even Wes, who had become an important part of their team.

As the day wrapped up, Mr. Matt approached the boys, clapping them on their shoulders. "You boys did well today. I'm proud of you."

Puck smiled. "Thanks, Mr. Matt. We couldn't have done it without all the help."

Mr. Matt nodded. "True, but remember, it was your idea that brought everyone together. That's the power of leadership and teamwork."

As the sun began to set over the river, Puck, Zane, Tad, and Wes stood together, their hearts full. They had learned something valuable that day, not just about organizing an event, but about themselves and each other.

DIRTY DOG
DUMPSTERS

Tides of Change

As a few years passed, the guys stayed in touch as best they could. However, with new hobbies, part-time jobs, college prep courses, and life changes, the gaps between their interactions grew longer. They still kept tabs on each other enough to know that Tad had started some college classes and had finally begun his adult dive training through the school. Zane completed his drone pilot's license and was now moving on to fixed-wing flight school.

Meanwhile, Puck became deeply involved in his community. He started working with public outreach programs in local churches and picked up several new hobbies. He learned how to play the guitar, began surfing, and took up camping. Puck marveled at the interconnectedness of everything. Music has tone, harmony, keys, and rhythm. Surfing relies on stance, foot placement, and rhythm that align with the rolling waves. Camping depends on balancing the elements to sustain life. When these were applied properly, Puck felt connected to God's creation and the people around him. The rhythm in the flow of water, the tone of creation, and the sync of teamwork in a group of campers all pointed to a greater design. But when there was a misstep, a wrong note, or a lack of sync, things could easily go wrong.

Every choice, whether a step, a tone, or an element, had a direct impact on the outcome. Creation has a natural order and flow, but human decisions have the power to work with or against that order. Puck embraced this design and wove it into all his passions.

Puck, now a strong outdoorsman, threw himself into studying for the written SCUBA test. His dedication was evident in every aspect of his preparation, from the way he pored over textbooks late into the night to his early morning practice sessions in the local pool. It was clear he had spent countless hours around the water, honing his skills and building a deep, intuitive understanding of the ocean's rhythms.

SCUBA diving, Puck discovered, was far more than just swimming underwater. It involved a complex interplay of math, science, reading, water safety, communication, and physics. As he delved deeper into each subject, Puck felt grateful for the time he had dedicated to learning over the years. Each piece of knowledge, every skill he had acquired, seemed to fit perfectly into place, preparing him for the next step in his training with Mr. Becker.

Reflecting on his journey, Puck realized that if he hadn't applied himself in all those areas, he might not have been able to move forward. It wasn't just about the physical skills-it was about mental discipline, problem-solving abilities, and the capacity to stay calm under pressure. All these qualities were crucial not only for SCUBA diving but also for whatever challenges lay ahead.

As he studied, Puck began to visualize his life and dreams as pieces of a grand puzzle. Each experience, each lesson learned, was a piece that needed to fit just right to complete the whole picture. But as the image became clearer, Puck realized something profound-the picture wasn't just about him. It included his family, his neighbors, and even the people he met along the way.

This realization gave Puck a new perspective. He began to understand that the more he poured into others, the more he gained in return, not in material rewards, but in meaningful growth. It wasn't just about what he could achieve but about how he could contribute. By sharing his strengths, he found opportunities to learn from others in areas where they excelled. This exchange of skills and knowledge formed a web of mutual support, becoming a source of inspiration and resilience. It reminded him of a body. Each part is designed to work together, each branch reaching into different areas of life to serve a specific purpose. Together, they moved forward, tackling challenges and taking the next steps toward growth and fulfillment.

Of course, the journey wasn't without setbacks. There were times when progress felt impossible, when the pieces of his dream seemed scattered and negativity threatened to derail him. Some people resisted change, unwilling to seek solutions or embrace better ways of doing things. Yet Puck came to see these moments as crucial. They weren't just obstacles; they were the fire that forged his determination. Through patience and persistence, he learned to navigate each situation one step at a time. Teamwork taught Puck the balance between leading and supporting, adapting and standing firm. Some moments called for flexibility, going with the flow, while others required the strength to stand like an unshakable rock against the current. Over time, Puck came to value the process, seeing it as the foundation upon which he could build his dreams and transform them into reality.

The Deep Dive In

As the day of the SCUBA exam approached, Puck felt a mix of nervousness and excitement. He was prepared. He knew the subject inside and out. He had put in the work day after day, and now he felt ready to face whatever challenges the test might bring along the way.

When the results came in, Puck discovered that his hard work had paid off. He passed the written SCUBA exam with flying colors, each correct answer a testament to his dedication and growth. As he held the results in his hands, Puck felt a surge of pride, not just in his achievement, but in the person he had become through this journey.

Yet even as he celebrated this milestone, Puck knew it was just the beginning. His mind raced with possibilities of what might come next. What new puzzles would he solve? What adventures awaited him beneath the waves? How would all of this prepare him for the greater purpose he sensed on the horizon?

With a mixture of excitement and determination, Puck looked toward the future. He was eager for what came next, ready to dive into new challenges and opportunities. Whatever awaited him, he knew he was ready-not just armed with his newfound skills, but fortified by the strength of character he had honed during his journey.

DIVE PLANS
1. Recon
2. Navigation
3. Descent
4. Search
5. Recovery
6. Ascent
7. Debrief
DIVER
EXAM COMPLETE
NEXT CHAPTER

With the written test behind him, Puck eagerly stepped into the next phase of his journey: pool training with Mr. Becker. This stage was critical, requiring him to master a wide array of diving skills before venturing into open water.

Standing by the edge of the shimmering pool, Puck adjusted the straps on his futuristic SCUBA suit, a suit that looked like it belonged in a science fiction movie. Memories of Mr. Becker's garage flooded back: the rows of mysterious and intricate equipment, some labeled with names he didn't recognize and others that seemed almost experimental. Back then, he had been in awe.

Mr. Becker didn't hold back. Over the weeks, Puck trained with every type of gear imaginable. He started with classic setups, replicas of the equipment used by the original Navy frogmen, heavy and rugged, built for endurance. Then came modern SCUBA systems: lightweight tanks, advanced regulators, and streamlined designs. But it didn't stop there.

"Today, we're trying something special," Mr. Becker said one morning, unveiling a compact rebreather that looked like it had been pulled from the future. "This is cutting-edge. It's not something you'll see on a recreational dive. Let's see how you handle it."

Puck practiced with gear designed for deep-sea exploration, cold-water diving, and even a prototype suit embedded with technology that monitored his vitals and adjusted buoyancy automatically. Some pieces felt like relics of a bygone era, while others seemed too advanced to be real. Each setup came with unique challenges and lessons, forcing Puck to adapt quickly and trust his growing skills.

In the water, Puck mastered breathing techniques, learned to stay calm under pressure, and practiced removing and reassembling his gear while submerged. He honed his navigation skills, learned emergency responses, and even trained for zero-visibility scenarios.

As Puck swam laps and performed underwater maneuvers, Mr. Becker would occasionally throw in surprises: a sudden simulated emergency or a switch to a new, unfamiliar piece of equipment.

By the time the pool sessions neared their end, Puck realized he wasn't just learning to dive-he was being prepared for a world few ever experienced.

Puck's final training took place in an enormous rock quarry, its cold depths filled with crystal-clear, eerily still water that concealed countless hidden secrets. As he descended, his senses came alive. The water was more than a space to explore; it was a world that seemed to stretch infinitely, surrounding him with the whispers of mysteries long buried. He swam alongside darting bass and scuttling crayfish, their fleeting movements barely rippling the quiet underwater realm.

Below, ghostly outlines of a sunken airplane and an old truck emerged-relics frozen in time-beckoning him closer with the promise of untold stories. In that moment, awe overwhelmed him; his mind reeled with the possibilities that lay hidden in these still waters.

Other divers moved ahead, silently communicating through graceful hand signals, a vital, unspoken language beneath the surface that guided one another toward new discoveries. Puck let them drift farther ahead, wanting to savor this moment of solitude. This was it, the very thing he had dreamed of, trained for, and imagined. The water embraced him, and with every breath he took, the line between dream and reality blurred.

In the stillness, it struck him: as if he had awakened from a dream, the vast unknown stretched out before him, waiting to be explored.

After completing his intense training, Puck proudly earned his SCUBA certification, a pivotal step toward his dream. He celebrated by diving into the deep end of Starlight Cove. The familiar waters felt alive with possibilities, stirring his imagination.

Eager to push his limits, Puck ventured into shadowy ponds and swamps, testing his skills with the different kinds of gear Mr. Becker asked him to try. The water was murky and mysterious, stretched before him like an uncharted world, thick with secrets yet to be uncovered. Each dive felt like stepping into the unknown. The surface above faded into silence as his gear drew him deeper. He sensed something extraordinary-this wasn't just a dream anymore; it was his new reality.

As he swam, the dream that had driven him felt almost tangible, as if the echoes of those who had supported him were with him in the water. Their presence lingered, as though they were part of his journey and connected him to the vast world beneath.

Yet beneath that connection, a deeper pull stirred- a feeling that something was still missing, something he couldn't quite define. It whispered of hidden mysteries and uncharted depths, urging him onward. Whatever it was, it fueled his passion to dive further, to discover what lay beneath the surface-and what it might reveal.

He plunged into rivers where swift currents tugged at him, surrounded by schools of fish darting like tiny arrows through the water. No longer just imagining these moments, Puck was now living them. As he explored, he learned to read the flow of the river, adjusting his movements to glide effortlessly with the current. Each dive sharpened his skills and gave him an opportunity to develop his God-given talents.
With every plunge, Puck mastered the art of underwater navigation, discovering hidden paths through submerged forests and weaving around rocks with the precision of a creature born to the depths. His world was no longer confined to dreams-the rush of the water, the tug of the current, and the thrill of exploration were all real, intensifying with every challenge he conquered.

Puck always took time to observe the smallest creatures in their natural environment. Each critter was fully functional, perfectly designed for its surroundings, and fascinating to watch in action. As his skills progressed during this stage, so did his appreciation for all of creation. He considered how his habitat and the underwater world's habitat were separate yet connected, impacting each other. Puck felt blessed to experience this environment and all its intricate details, even if his time in the aquatic world was limited each day.

Diving had rules-rules based on facts and the laws of nature. The deepest dive always had to be completed first each day. Time limits were determined by the amount of compressed air he breathed at different depths and how quickly he could return to the surface. A single violation of these principles could cause major problems during a dive. These rules sustained life. Puck kept these guidelines in his mind and heart at all times. They were not meant to contain him; they were meant to keep him safe and alive. This was the freedom to go where others could not follow.

In the vast oceans, coral reefs stretched out like shimmering underwater cities, vibrant with life. Puck's heart raced as he swam alongside colorful schools of fish, their synchronized movements a blur of brilliance. Gliding through the mysterious aquatic landscapes, he felt the thrill of discovery with each dive, eager for the next shipwreck or hidden marvel waiting beneath the surface.

But amid the beauty, Puck noticed unsettling evidence that the surface world had seeped into the deep. Man-made relics lie forgotten on the ocean floor. Some told the story of human history-ancient trade vessels and remnants of past wars. Others, like plastic debris and fiberglass wreckage, were reminders of carelessness and neglect. The older wrecks, made of wood and metal, had become part of the ecosystem, transformed into shelter for marine life. In contrast, the newer debris disrupted the balance, choking out life rather than fostering it.

Puck's thoughts stirred. God gave us this world to steward, yet we are failing not just in caring for creation, but in something far greater. The deeper he looked, the more he realized this wasn't just about the ocean. The world itself was unraveling. Advancements meant to improve life had instead led to destruction, and human wisdom had proven powerless to fix the mess.

He saw the same truth reflected in himself. Sin had corrupted everything both within and around him. The evidence was everywhere. If the world was breaking, it wasn't just the environment; it was people, their hearts, their choices. No amount of human effort could fix what only God could redeem. In 1 John 5, hope wasn't found in progress but in a Savior. True restoration of the world, of hearts, of purpose was only possible through Christ. Faith in Him was the first step, and as each step was taken, God would direct the path.

As the years passed, Puck honed his skills, completed college, and continued to help others whenever he could. Yet no matter how full his life became, he always found time to return to the water. Whether exploring remote dive spots around the globe or seeking the familiar sanctuary of Starlight Cove, the water called to him. It was here, beneath the surface, that he felt most at home-where every breath held a promise of discovery and a quiet reminder of his journey.

Each dive into the tranquil depths of the cove was like stepping into a sacred space. As the cool blue waters embraced him, Puck felt his mind clear, and his senses sharpen. He reflected on the challenges he had faced, the lessons he had learned, and the dreams born in this very place. Starlight Cove had always been untouched by the reckless hand of man; a pristine world where nature flourished as it was meant to.

But today, something was different as he moved through the serene waters; thoughts of the wider world intruded. The rivers and oceans that were scarred by neglect- these places that weren't as fortunate as Starlight Cove. He remembered the team that had come together to restore the Old Black Water River, a group united by a shared purpose, working not for themselves, but for the good of something greater. It had been the start of something.

Beneath the surface of the cove, the weight of his mission pressed against his chest, stronger than ever before. He could no longer stay submerged in these peaceful waters, pretending that the outside world didn't need the same care. For the first time, the water no longer called him to stay. Instead, it urged him to rise. With a powerful kick, Puck broke the surface. The sun glistened on the water as he pulled off his mask, taking in a deep breath of air. He had emerged not just from the cove, but from the path that had shaped him-no longer just a diver, but a protector. A leader. The Frogman.

Salvaging Hope

Puck wasted no time after his revelation at Starlight Cove. He quickly called Rudy and Whit from Wounded Nature, as well as Brox and Ryan from Black Water Dredging. "Meet me at the marina," he urged, the urgency clear in his voice. "We need to start cleaning up more than just the old Black Water River. It's time to get the whole area free of debris. Let's restore this place."

The response was immediate. Mr. Matt, who had always supported their efforts, reached out to two more trusted allies- Mr. Derrick and Mr. Jordan. Mr. Arron showed up with his dumpsters and offered to help. The team began to assemble, committed to the mission ahead.

Partially submerged fiberglass vessels stood as silent eyesores along the shoreline- remnants of neglect, their sharp edges peeking out of the water like scars on the landscape.

"This fiberglass breakdown is bad news," Rudy muttered as he surveyed the scene. "It's polluting the waters, getting into the fish and the shellfish. It's a ticking time bomb for marine life."

Whit nodded, adding, "We're doing more harm than good with this stuff. Time to change that."

Mr. Derrick surveyed the wreckage with an experienced eye. "I'll bring the excavator and haul these vessels out. They won't know what hit them."

Brox grinned. "My crew's ready to hit every site. We'll load those wrecks onto the barge in no time. I've got Ryan, the best trackhoe operator you've ever seen. Heck, between him and Mr. Derrick, those two could flip quarters with the buckets!"

Ryan gave a modest nod, but his smile said he was up for the challenge.

Mr. Jordan chimed in, "Bring them to me in one piece or a hundred, and I'll strap them down. The Solid Waste Authority is still on board for this cleanup effort. I'll haul them out of there."

With the plan set, the team wasted no time. By dawn the following day, they were already in action. Rudy, Whit, and Puck dove in, identifying the worst vessels first. Puck swiftly wrapped straps around the hulls while Rudy and Whit secured the lines. Above, Brox's crew maneuvered debris with precision. Ryan, operating the track hoe with skill, lifted the wreckage and loaded it onto the barge.

Brox grinned. "Told you Ryan's the best. We're setting a record today!"

Mr. Matt towed smaller vessels, keeping the momentum going. "Let's keep it up, guys!" he urged. With each haul, the area began to transform, becoming cleaner and more pristine. Piece by piece, they restored the waterway, knowing their work was making a real difference.

By midafternoon, they had surpassed their goal. Mr. Derrick loaded floating vessels onto flatbed trailers and placed pieces of others into bins. Mr. Jordan, tying down the final load, called out, "That's it! We've cleared more derelict vessels than ever before!"

As the team gathered, exhausted but triumphant, Puck gazed over the cleared waters, filled with hope. They had achieved more than just a cleanup; it was the start of something bigger. Watching the barge sail away, Puck knew this was only the beginning.

"Next time, we go even bigger," he said, and the team nodded, ready for the next challenge. The Frogman had emerged, and their mission was far from over.

As Puck loaded his gear and everyone said their goodbyes, he overheard Mr. Matt and Mr. Derrick speaking in low voices.

"We need to tell Hardee he's ready," Mr. Matt said. "It's time to move forward."

Puck paused, wondering what they meant, but before he could ask, they climbed into their trucks and departed.

OUTPOST
BLACKWATER DREDGING

The Tide Returns

Then, one day, an underwater pipe became clogged with mud and debris. Mr. Derrick hurriedly briefed Puck on the emergency. "This is urgent-we need your help. Mr. Becker's out of town on business!"

Determined, Puck grabbed his gear and rushed to meet Derrick. As he suited up, a nagging thought surfaced: Derrick knows Becker, too. What is going on here? He shook off the questions and dove into the water, his instincts guiding him toward the enormous pipe.

As soon as he reached it, he knew something was off. This was no ordinary drainage pipe; it was larger and more natural, like a tunnel, as if designed for more than just runoff. The structure felt deliberate, ancient, even as though it had a purpose that had been hidden or forgotten over time. Mud and debris caked the entrance, making his task grueling. His pulse quickened. This was no accident.

Finally, with one last powerful pull, the blockage gave way. The water surged through in a rush, flooding the tunnel with life once again. As Puck surfaced, he knew there was something about the moment that felt larger than the job he had just completed.

It wasn't just water he had released; it was a sign. A signal. The tide had returned not only to this forgotten tunnel but also to something much greater. Puck felt it in his bones. This wasn't just a cleanup mission. He was on the edge of a deeper mystery, one tied to Becker, Derrick, and something far bigger than himself.

The tide had indeed returned, and somehow, he was at the center of it. He felt the pull of something big on the horizon.

The next day, Puck received an urgent call from Derrick and headed to the marina to meet him. As they arrived simultaneously, Puck began loading his gear into Derrick's vehicle.

"It's a lost family heirloom," Derrick explained. "I got word that it's at the bottom of a deep lake."

From the deck of the ship store, Matt called out, "Puck, you and Derrick, be careful out there today. Dive smart and stay safe."

Puck waved back with a grin. "You bet, Mr. Matt. Want to come along?"

Matt shook his head. "I wish I could, but I'm short on help and working on a puzzle of sorts. Anyway, good luck with the recovery- and stay safe."

Puck and Derrick made their way to the lake. As they prepared the gear, Derrick pulled up a satellite view on his laptop.

"It should be right around here," he said, pointing to a spot on the image.

Puck suited up, the weight of his frogman gear familiar and reassuring. As he slipped into the water, the world above faded, replaced by the cool, eerie silence of the lake. The thermocline hit hard as he descended, making the bottom feel colder and more foreboding. The lakebed was a tangle of plants and jagged rocks-a submerged puzzle to navigate.

Then, through the murky silt and debris, Puck caught a glimmer. He moved closer, his hands steady, and retrieved the artifact-a strange yet familiar symbol etched into its surface.

When Puck surfaced, he handed it to Derrick.

"That's an interesting symbol," Puck said, studying the image of an octopus. "I love the design. It looks like one I found in Matt's attic a while back. You think they're connected?"

Derrick paused, his eyes lingering on the artifact. "It's very cool, Puck. We need to get it cleaned up and take it to someone who might know more."

Puck couldn't shake the feeling that this was more than just a family heirloom. Something about the symbol stirred his curiosity, hinting at deeper connections he was only beginning to understand.

Derrick's eyes narrowed. After a brief pause, he pulled out his phone.

"I'm calling Hardee; he'll want to hear about this," he muttered, stepping away for a moment.

Puck leaned against the dock railing, his mind still buzzing from the discovery. There was something about the artifact that felt ancient-but also strange- like it carried a hidden story. He had a growing sense that this wasn't just an ordinary recovery mission.

Derrick returned, his expression unreadable.

"Puck, Hardee's is on board with what we're doing, but this might be bigger than we first thought."

"What do you mean?" Puck asked, intrigued.

"You up for another dive?" Derrick said, packing the gear back into their bags with quick, deliberate movements.

Puck straightened up. "Yeah, but what's going on?"

"We've got a boat to catch. I'll explain on the way."

At the dock, a sleek boat idled in the water, its engine quietly thrumming.

"Just another dive, right?" Puck said. Yet even as he spoke, he knew it wasn't true. His instincts told him there was much more going on beneath the surface-literally.

As they boarded the boat and sped off into the open water, the wind whipping past them, Derrick leaned in closer.

"That artifact you found- it's part of a larger puzzle. And it's not the only one out there. This next stop involves a wreck. A downed plane off the coast, but it's connected. These items... they weren't just lost. They were hidden."

"Hidden?" Puck echoed, his mind racing. "By whom?"

"There are those who do not want to see us succeed," Derrick replied, his tone more guarded now. "But one thing's for sure: there are others out there looking for these artifacts too. That's why this dive is important. We need to move fast before someone else gets there."

Puck's grip tightened on the railing as the boat sliced through the waves, excitement and tension building in his chest. This wasn't just another recovery; something larger was at play, and he had the growing sense that he was only scratching the surface of a much deeper mystery.

Derrick's voice cut through the wind. "Keep your eyes open. If someone else is out there, they won't be friendly."

The gravity of the situation sank in. It wasn't just about recovering artifacts; it was about who else wanted them and why.

The boat slowed at the dive site, the engine's hum fading. "We're here," Derrick announced as the anchor splashed into the water.

Puck suited up in traditional black frogman gear. He nodded to Derrick, then backrolled over the side, slipping into the cool ocean.

As he descended, the shadowy outline of the warplane emerged from the blue-green depths, a ghostly remnant of the past. Puck scanned the area, unsure of what he should be looking for-Derrick hadn't given many details.

Then, out of the corner of his eye, Puck noticed movement. A sleek, unmanned submersible was approaching the wreck. It wasn't theirs.

Without hesitation, Puck swam toward a tangled fishing net caught in the wreck. Timing his move, he threw the net over the submersible, causing it to snag and stall.

With the threat disabled, Puck turned back to the wreck. His eyes landed on a small case wedged between some metal panels. As he pried it loose, he saw the same octopus emblem, the one from the artifact in the lake. This had to be what Derrick was after.

Puck secured the case, feeling its weight, both physical and symbolic, as he kicked upward toward the surface, the depths swirling with untold secrets.

As Puck resurfaced with the case, Mr. Derrick was already waiting at the edge of the boat.
"Another symbol like the others," said Puck as he handed the artifact up.
"Good work, Puck," Derrick replied, his tone more serious than before.
Puck climbed aboard the boat, but before he could share what had happened with the submersible, Derrick's phone rang. Puck recognized Mr. Hardee's voice. It was clear something bigger was happening.
After hanging up, Derrick turned to Puck. "We've got another mission. There's an old work train submerged in the Old Black Water River. This time, we need the whole thing, and Brox is already bringing the barge to haul it out."
Puck wiped the water from his face, sensing the growing urgency. "What's the catch?" he asked.
Derrick's expression tightened. "A territorial gator, big one. Special Agent Austin from Coast Guard Environmental is en route to assist. You've worked with Brox before; you up for it?"
Puck's pulse quickened. He glanced again at the octopus symbol, feeling its strange pull. "I'm in. The team's coming back together, and this symbol means something important. Just tell me what needs to be done."
Derrick nodded. "Good. This isn't just about the artifact- it's a key to something much bigger. We'll meet the rest of the team at dawn. Brox and Ryan need ten hours to get the barge on the scene up the Old Black Water River. Get a meal and a good night's rest. We've had a full day's work, and we're looking at another long day tomorrow."
As the boat rocked gently beneath him, Puck looked out over the darkening water, knowing that whatever waited in those gator-infested depths was only the start of something far larger and far more dangerous than he could have imagined.

The sun was beginning to rise the next morning, casting an orange glow over the misty waters of the Old Black Water River. Puck stood at the riverbank, surveying the scene. Brox's barge was already anchored near the shore, with Ryan perched in the cab of his massive excavator. The roar of the tugboat's engine hummed in the background, its thick ropes securing it to the barge. They climbed on board.

Agent Austin from the Coast Guard gave Puck a nod as he stepped aboard. "You must be Puck," Austin said. "We've heard a lot about your cleanups and dives. You ready for this?"

Puck grinned. "I've been ready."

Just then, Puck spotted Mr. Hardee approaching with Derrick. This was the first time they had met in person, but Puck could tell by Hardee's demeanor that he meant business. He extended his hand. "Mr. Hardee, right?"

"That's me," Hardee replied, gripping Puck's hand firmly. "Glad to have you on board. This situation's more delicate than we thought-we need the entire train intact, and that gator isn't going anywhere soon. But here's some good news: I've secured permission from the public water company. They own this property, and they're big supporters of our work. They want to see this work train restored after we're done. History lies buried beneath the surface, waiting to be uncovered."

Hardee glanced at Derrick. "I've got Jordan and Jones on the way. You'll like Jones; he's a genius with metal restoration. He'll know how to handle the rest once we get it out of the water. We've got to move quickly, though. Timing is everything, especially with that gator on patrol."

Puck felt a new wave of responsibility. The team was counting on him not just for the dive but to make sure the plan worked without a hitch. He nodded, glancing at the dark waters ahead. "Let's get to work."

Puck glanced at the dark water where the gator lurked. He'd faced tricky situations before, but this was a different kind of challenge.

"I've got an idea," Puck said. "Ryan, you think you can trickle water from the trackhoe bucket?"

Ryan, leaning out of the cab, raised an eyebrow. "Water? Sure, but what are you thinking?"

"If we create a distraction with the water, the gator might focus on that, giving me a window to slip in. Once I'm in, I'll hook up the chains to the train so we can pull it out in one piece."

Brox, standing nearby with his arms crossed, chuckled. "We've done crazier things, Puck. You think that'll work?"

"I do," Puck replied confidently, recalling how they'd tackled tough projects before. "But we'll need to time it right."

Mr. Hardee nodded. "Sounds like the best plan we've got. Let's do it."

Ryan fired up the trackhoe, slowly lifting the bucket and dipping it into the river. As water began to trickle from it, the team held their breath, watching the gator focus on the distraction.

"Now's your chance," Austin whispered, his eyes scanning the water.

Puck slipped into the river, his movements quick and deliberate. The water was murky, but he could see the outline of the sunken train below. As the bucket splashed steady streams of water, Puck caught a shadow still moving toward the distraction.

He swam toward the train, carrying the chain in one hand. His heart raced as he reached the front of the submerged engine, fastening the chain to the couplings as quickly as possible.

Back on the barge, Brox and Agent Austin kept a close eye on the water, waiting for Puck's signal. After what felt like an eternity, Puck resurfaced, holding up a hand.

"We're hooked! Pull it out!"

Ryan, with practiced precision, maneuvered the track hoe, and the chains tightened. Slowly, the rusted frame of the train began to emerge from the water, dripping and creaking as it was lifted onto the barge. As the train settled onto the deck, everyone breathed a sigh of relief.

After a thorough inspection, Agent Austin gave a nod of approval. "It meets all environmental standards and is free of contamination in my book. We're clear to proceed as planned. Nice work, Puck!"

Brox laughed, wiping sweat from his brow. "You've got guts, Puck. I'll give you that."

Just then, the sound of a truck approaching the shoreline drew their attention. Mr. Jordan and Mr. Jones, who were set to handle the transport and restoration, stepped out of the vehicle.

"Sorry, we're late," Mr. Jordan called out, adjusting his cap. "We ran into a strange traffic delay and needed law enforcement to clear it up."

Mr. Jones, examining the train from a distance, nodded. "Good thing we made it, though. We've got some work ahead of us. We'll load up the train and get it ready for transport. Looks like this old workhorse has seen better days, but it's important to preserve this piece of history for the community."

Mr. Jordan added, "This isn't just a restoration; it's a marvel of engineering. Out of that design came years of hard work from this beauty. It takes input to achieve output. This train's got a story to tell, and it's going to be a part of that legacy."

1920

Converging Tides: The Forge

The warm afternoon sun cast long shadows over the Old Black Water River, and the air buzzed with the sound of cicadas. As the rusted train was secured on the flatbed of Mr. Jordan's tow truck, the group gathered nearby. Puck stood beside Mr. Hardee and Mr. Derrick, still processing the intense dive he had just completed.

Brox leaned against the truck, wiping dirt from his hands.

"This train must have been something back in the day," he muttered. "But if what you're saying is true, it's more than just a piece of history."

Mr. Hardee, his face a mix of urgency and resolve, nodded. "You're right, Brox. This train holds more than meets the eye. The artifacts we've recovered are fragments of a much larger mission-one started by Team TIDES."

Puck, intrigued, took in Mr. Hardee's words. "Team TIDES?" he asked, his voice steady but curious. "Can you share more? That octopus symbol was on a bottle in Mr. Matt's shop. How does that fit in?"

Before Mr. Hardee could respond, the distant hum of an approaching vehicle caught their attention. Zane's car pulled up, kicking up dust as it stopped. He stepped out, his eyes immediately finding Puck. A grin spread across his face.

"Puck!" Zane called out, walking over. "Guess I'm not too late, huh?"

Puck smiled, clapping Zane on the shoulder. "Not at all. Glad you're here."

The two friends, who had shared countless memories at Starlight Cove, exchanged a knowing look, both now aware of how far they'd come and excited for what was next. But the reunion wasn't over. A second car rolled in, and when the door opened, Tad stepped out.

Puck's eyes widened in disbelief. It had been years since he had last seen Tad.

"Tad?" Puck called out, unable to hide his surprise.

Tad smiled as he walked toward him. "It's been a long time, but I heard you've been busy with all this... well, so have I! I told you we would be frogmen." He extended his hand, and Puck grasped it. It was a reunion long overdue.

Mr. Hardee observed the exchange before speaking up, including Zane and Tad in the conversation. "I wanted both of you here for a reason. This isn't just a mission; it's a calling. Team TIDES was a group of people dedicated to building communities. They were pilots, frogmen, investors, teachers, government workers, and ordinary citizens who focused on core values in life. They worked together, utilizing teamwork, integrity, dedication, excellence, and service. Zane, you're a descendant of the original Team TIDES pilot. Tad and Puck, you both have family members who were part of the original team. You all are essential to the team's future."

Zane, intrigued but serious, nodded. "I knew something was up. You've had me flying crews to some pretty remote places, but I didn't realize it was connected to our history."

Puck, still processing the revelations, looked at Mr. Hardee. "So, we're all tied to this legacy- Team TIDES?"

Mr. Hardee nodded. "Yes. You've been part of it from the beginning, even if you didn't realize it. The missions are covert for security, but the purpose of Team TIDES is no secret. You all exhibit the core values, and those qualities are contagious. But now, I need to show you something. It's time you fully understand what we're up against. You are invited to a facility where we will be taking the train so we can tell you what we know. The choice is always up to you."

Mr. Hardee turned to the group. "Normally, we'd use an Octopod transport from Mr. Matt's shop, but for this, we need to take the train by truck." His voice lowered. "This is classified. Once we reach the facility, you'll understand why."

The air buzzed with anticipation as they piled into the vehicles. The train, now firmly strapped down, rumbled as the convoy set off. The drive wasn't long- about an hour- but the landscape shifted from the winding roads along the river to dense forests. Eventually, they approached the facility, camouflaged within the natural surroundings. The gate slid open as Mr. Jordan drove through, revealing a state-of-the-art compound hidden in plain sight. It resembled a covert government installation, blending high-tech security with the natural environment.

Mr. Hardee looked back at the group as they exited the vehicles. "Welcome to the Forge, where every tool, plan, and strategy is crafted with precision to protect what matters most, people, to fight the eternal battle between light and darkness."

Puck, Zane, and Tad exchanged glances, their eyes wide with amazement. The compound featured numerous buildings equipped with advanced technology, all surrounded by shimmering lakes. As Mr. Hardee led them toward the main facility, the sound of a train being unloaded echoed in the background.

"We have a lot to discuss and someone for you to meet," he said. "Our science engineer has been working closely with us. Her relative was an inventor who created the first frogman gear for the original team and the plane from which Puck recovered an artifact."

As they walked, he continued, "They also invented the train to serve the local community's needs and developed a highly effective cutting blade powered by high-pressure water. That device was used to create the underwater tunnels, among other things; we'll cover soon enough."

WELCOME

"Team TIDES was more than just a group-it was a movement," Mr. Hardee began, his voice steady but charged with the weight of history. "They stood for values that some people have lost over the years. They protected each other, helped people succeed, safeguarded the environment, and showed respect. They were positive influencers, stewards of what had been entrusted to them. They followed the light to guide their path, using Ephesians 5:11." He paused, letting everyone recall the verse. "But over time, they faced relentless opposition, forces that sought to undo everything for which they stood. This opposition, known as RIPTIDE, is a group of dissenters driven by personal gain, thriving on negativity, pollution, selfishness, and the destruction of our heritage. They've been attempting to sabotage us, disrupting our missions, including the incident with the plane and submersible, and even the traffic jam that delayed Mr. Jordan and Mr. Jones. Puck, even your basic suits have some exceptional upgrades."

Mr. Hardee continued, "That wasn't just any pipe you cleared, Puck. It's part of an underground supply line for clean hydropower and a secret transportation route for elite frogmen; one entrance is at Matt's shop. RIPTIDE targeted it to stop us. Worse, they've captured Mr. Becker, and he's being held at their underwater base, which explains his absence."

The room fell into a tense silence, but Puck broke through the weight of Mr. Hardee's words.

"The bottle in the attic... it was part of this, wasn't it?" His voice grew more certain. "That bottle unlocked the map. Matt and I found the first key."

Mr. Hardee's eyes met Puck's, a flicker of pride in his gaze. "Yes, Puck. You and Matt discovered the first clue. You've been leading us toward the answers all along. The light shines in the darkness and uncovers the path ahead."

As Puck and Matt were finishing up one evening, Matt accidentally knocked the bottle over. The light from his desk lamp pierced through the green glass, projecting an intricate map onto the wall. That map, as it turned out, was our first real clue-the key that led us to the location of the artifacts.

Puck's brow furrowed as he replayed the moment. "Why did the original team have to hide the artifacts? Shouldn't those core values stand the test of time? How could something so good be threatened by a negative force?"

Mr. Hardee leaned forward, his expression serious. "Those are the answers we're hoping to uncover soon. But even in the darkest hours of the night, the moon reflects the true light of the sun. Starlight can take years to reach Earth. So, there is a light in the past that shines into the future. These artifacts are similar to the moon shape behind the octopus symbol."

He paused, letting the concept settle in. "We know that the original team placed these artifacts, the plane, the train, as deliberate pieces of a puzzle for us to find. But right now, the most important piece is you. You've all grown tremendously, and our success hinges on how we continue to grow as a team."

Mr. Hardee scanned the room, his voice steady. "This isn't just a job-it's a calling. But it comes with substantial rewards. You'll have access to every resource, every piece of gear or technology needed to excel. Whatever it takes to fulfill your role in Team TIDES will be at your disposal."

The energy in the room shifted, electric with newfound purpose. Enthusiastic voices filled the air: "I'm all in! "Where do I sign up? "Let's do this! "Count me in!"

It was clear that the group was ready to embrace the mission, united in their commitment to Team TIDES and the mysteries still waiting to be uncovered.

"Then that's settled," Mr. Hardee said with a satisfied nod. "Welcome to the team!"

Mr. Hardee turned to address the group, a proud smile on his face. "Team TIDES, it's time to meet the mastermind behind much of what you'll see today, our chief project engineer, Dr. Ebbstone, though most of us call her Dr. E."

The woman standing nearby stepped forward, her presence radiating energy and purpose. "Finally!" she said with a grin. "I've been waiting for this. Now listen up-I talk fast, I move faster, and there's no time for second-guessing. Choppa-choppa, let's go!"

She waved them forward briskly, her tone playful but commanding. With that, Dr. E spun on her heel and strode down a long corridor, her quick pace leaving the group scrambling to keep up. The hall stretched ahead like a gateway to another world, every step filled with growing anticipation.

When they reached the end, she pressed her palm to a glowing panel, and the door slid open with a faint hum. The sight beyond was staggering. The room, if it could even be called that, was massive, more complex than a single space. Branching hallways led to specialized zones, each bursting with advanced technology. A low murmur of awe rippled through the group.

"Welcome," Dr. E said, spreading her arms as if presenting a masterpiece. "To the Vaultrium."

The word seemed to hang in the air, as impressive as the space itself. Zane's eyes darted to the aerospace corridor, where sleek planes and drones lined the walls, ready for deployment. Nearby, a corridor showcased amphibious vehicles, boats, and aquatic gear, the latter glistening as if still wet. Another path led to an arsenal of vehicles, ATVs, trucks, and even futuristic cars. To the far left, robotic systems and super suits stood on display, each one a testament to cutting-edge innovation.

Dr. E's voice carried effortlessly through the vast chamber. "This is more than a lab. It's a culmination of partnerships, innovation, and a shared vision. Everything here serves a purpose-from the smallest drone to the most advanced suit. It's all yours- every tool, every resource. You're not just a team anymore; you're the stewards of what comes next."

She paused for a moment. Then, with a mischievous smile, she added, "And now that you're here, it's time to see what the future looks like."

With a wave of her hand, Dr. E led them into the central engineering hub, where a holographic console glowed in the dim light.

Echo Sync: Amphibious Gear-Up

Dr. E tapped the holographic console, and the room sprang to life. Sleek, high-tech suits appeared as though on display in a futuristic gallery. Her eyes sparkled with excitement as she addressed the team.

"Welcome to the next generation of amphibious technology: Echo Sync Amphibious Technology, or E.S.A.T. It's far more advanced than the prototype you tried in Echo Sync mode in Becker's garage, Puck. Sorry about that! I was nine and had only been designing for a year.

"Anyway, these suits, the aircraft, and the drones aren't just tools; they're extensions of you in the field. Each piece has been custom-tuned to enhance your abilities, revolutionizing strength, agility, flight, underwater navigation, and speed."

Puck exchanged an eager glance with Tad as Dr. E gestured toward the frogman suits.

"These? They're equipped with solar-powered nanobots that activate stealth in Hyper-Realistic Amphibious Mode, or H.R.A.M. You'll move as one with the water, with enhanced speed, agility, and camouflage that echoes every motion, adapting in real time. They naturally adjust to your environmental needs.

"The camouflage isn't just for blending into an environment-you could appear older, younger, or even like an average bystander. In high-stakes situations, it's a lifesaver. Environmental elements trigger the suit to adapt and switch output modes. As you and the team activate the nanobots, they create what you ask them to through sync, but the bots also adjust to your needs. It's all about team communication."

Austin raised his hand, eyes wide. "Wait, we can change these suits by communicating with the bots? Just like that?"

Dr. E smirked. "Exactly. Think of it as the ultimate chameleon suit-but on demand. And there's more: each suit's holographic mode lets you create distractions, project decoys, or communicate across areas where traditional tech can't.

"Every piece- aircraft, drones, frogman gear, flight suits, and transport pods syncs seamlessly. The tech amplifies each component, transforming your teamwork into a fluid network. It enhances your senses and shares that information with the entire team. We also added some neat features you'll discover soon."

Puck and Tad shared a grin, feeling the thrill of endless possibilities beyond anything they'd imagined.

NANOBOT SYNCHRONIZATION
NETWORK
ADAPTIVE CAMOUFLAGE
LAYER
HYDRODYNAMIC OPTIMIZATION
CAEIBQATION
SPECTRUM CAMOUFLAGE
PROPULSION SYSTEMS
NEXT SUIT ROTA
TACTICAL EXO-A

Dr. E shifted her focus to Zane. "Your plane can convert to underwater mode when needed."
Zane's eyes lit up. "So, I could fly underwater if necessary?"
"Exactly." Dr. E nodded. "In the air, it can fly almost silently and has a built-in hover mode. If you ever need to, let's say, disrupt something, it can release sound waves powerful enough to disorient without causing permanent harm."
Austin, who had been trying to keep up with Dr. E's rapid pace, blinked. "Wait, did you say sound waves? What are we talking about here, like a sonic boom?"
Dr. E paused mid-speech, noticing the confused look. "Oh, did I lose you? Sorry! Imagine this: you're mid-flight, then bam, you need to throw off a threat. A pulse of sound disorients, confuses, and gives you time to escape or regroup. Got it now?"
Austin gave a slow nod.
The whole team chuckled as Dr. E grinned. "Don't worry, you'll get a chance to test it all out soon."
She then turned to the drones. "And let's not forget these. Your drones? They're not just extra eyes; they're packed with many of the same features as your suits and Zane's plane. You'll use them for reconnaissance, communication, and even underwater missions. They've got camouflage, holographic projections, and non-lethal tools-everything from EMP bursts to inking and sticky goo traps. No one will see them coming.
"All of the suits condense into this TIDES watch for rapid deployment of the nanobots. You only need one watch to generate any of these suits and construct various drones, hoverboards, and more. Here you go," Dr. E said, handing everyone a watch. "Over there is a group of different Octopods with the same capabilities and more. We use them to transport people needing medical attention and extra gear. They sync, and you can operate them through remote holographic commands, just like your drones.
"Now try on your TIDES watches-your suits will adapt automatically."

SYSTEM INTEGRITY
NANITE RESERVE: 100
TIDES NANOBAND SYSTEMS
FULL-SPECTRUM SUIT GENERATION
STANDBY MODE
AWAITING SYNCHRONIZATION

Puck and Tad could barely contain their excitement as they activated their watches and formed their suits, feeling the nanobots spark to life. Zane readied his gear, already envisioning how his new flight suit would look-and the drones, which would change the game.

As Dr. E called after them, "Don't forget H.R.A.M.-it'll make all the difference," the team scattered to their specialized stations.

Austin constructed a hoverboard, launched his drone, and linked into the comms network. His drone used sensors to detect any ecosystem disturbances around the team.

Derrick suited up, fine-tuning communications and syncing with his drone, ensuring their encrypted signals remained untraceable.

Matt suited up and headed to the octopod transport, while Jordan focused on preparing the heavier equipment. Jones, always focused, busied himself with engineering the suit diagnostics. Using his suit, he scanned the train, pinpointed the artifact locations, and uploaded the data to the base server.

Zane headed to his plane, powering it up. The sound of the engine was barely more than a whisper in the wind as he brought it into a hover. His mind buzzed with possibilities as he tested the stealth mode, feeling the thrill of the aircraft disappearing into the sky.

Meanwhile, Tad and Puck dove into the water tunnel, their suits syncing perfectly with the currents. They moved with blinding speed, like living shadows, leaving faint trails of bubbles in their wake. Their suits maintained an echo-like connection, relaying signals to each other seamlessly as they powered forward, ready for anything.

TIDES NANOBAND SYSTEMS
FULL-SPECTRUM SUIT GENERATION
ANDBY MODE
WAITING SYNCHRONIZATION

The thrill of the gear-up moment electrified the group. Even though they were testing and training, the seriousness of their mission ahead lingered.

Back at the base, Dr. E activated her suit and hailed everyone on comms. "All right, team, listen up! You have ten minutes to try different suit generations, then I want you all back at the Vaultrium. We've got to be sharp when we go in for Mr. Becker. Work as a team, use your gear, and remember, the tech is only as good as the one using it. It's designed that way."

Puck felt a surge of confidence as he surfaced from the water. "This is incredible."

Zane, still up in the sky, chimed in over comms. "Copy that."

As the countdown ticked down, Mr. Hardee suited up and synced with the team. "Before you get too far out, we need to talk about RIPTIDE. They've been getting reckless lately. They managed to steal some high-level tech from a downtown warehouse, a prototype we were working on. If we don't get it back soon, there's no telling what they'll do with it."

Puck exchanged a worried glance with Tad. "What kind of tech?"

Hardee's jaw tightened. "Let's just say if RIPTIDE figures it out, they'll be able to gain the upper hand. We need to be on top of our game. Okay, TIDES, align!"

Just like that, Hardee's voice echoed through their super-tech, the command creating a ripple of connection between them. The HUDs pulsed to life, each suit in sync, and the team felt the flow shift. They weren't just linked up; they were in perfect rhythm, moving as one current.

Puck and Tad were the first to appear. They shot through the underwater transport tunnel like two streamlined shadows, emerging from the tunnel entrance with precision. As they launched into the Vaultrium, they struck poses, water shedding off their suits, which flickered and morphed into stealth mode.

"How's that for a synchronized entrance?" Tad quipped, giving Puck a playful nudge.

Zane arrived next. His aircraft swooped into hover mode above the Vaultrium's open expanse, and he launched himself out of the cockpit, gliding to the floor in his custom flight suit. The aircraft held steady, hovering above the team like a silent guardian.

One by one, the rest of the team entered. Mr. Jones emerged from an invisible camouflage state, appearing almost out of thin air with a sly grin.

"Guess this suit works as advertised."

Just then, Derrick rolled in on a tactical ATV, its quiet engine humming as he smoothly parked beside the group. Not far behind him, Mr. Jordan's truck drove into the Vaultrium with a confident presence.

"Look, Mom, no hands," he said, chuckling as he joined the lineup using sync mode to operate the vehicle.

Austin arrived, gliding on a hoverboard designed like a sleek, futuristic surfboard.

"Figured I'd bring something practical," he said, smirking as he expertly dismounted. "This baby's perfect for investigating environmental spills-multi-terrain, silent mode, and-wait for it-self-cleaning."

Austin deconstructed the hoverboard, and the nanos converged with his suit.

Just as they gathered, a figure appeared across the room-an unfamiliar face dressed in civilian attire. The team exchanged confused glances, unsure who the stranger was.

Tad broke the silence. "Uh, who's this guy?"
The figure smirked and tilted his head. "Mr. Hardee," he said coolly, "but I am not here. Actually, I'm over here."
The team exchanged puzzled looks as they located a blinking icon in their HUDs-a sleek, holographic symbol resembling an eye within a shield, subtly pulsing to signify "True Identity."

Mr. Hardee's voice came through again, amused. "Heads up, team-when you see this icon, it means a team member is in disguise or projecting a hologram. Select it now to reveal my actual position."

They engaged the icon, and the real Mr. Hardee materialized beside them. His disguise flickered off, revealing his true self, flanked by a pair of drones that had carried him in. The team turned, catching the glimmer of amusement in his eyes as he took his place in the lineup.

Finally, the soft hum of a quiet engine filled the space, and Matt rolled in on a nearly soundless, state-of-the-art motorcycle. He pulled to a stop, kicking down the stand as he admired the vehicle.
"You know," he said, grinning as he removed his helmet, "I could get used to this."

The team stood assembled, a force of cutting-edge tech and expertise, each member embodying their gear's sleek design. With every suit and skill in sync, the command was clear, but the purpose was even clearer: get Mr. Becker back, no matter the odds. Each felt a surge of purpose; they were TIDES, ready to shift the flow.

VAULTRIUM
TEAM TIDES
MARSHALL
DAVIS
PIERCE
HARRISON
VAULTRIUM

As the team gathered in the main hall after a long day, they took in the familiar hum of the surrounding technology. Mr. Hardee stood at the front. A calm presence amidst their energy, watching as everyone settled down. He cleared his throat, capturing their attention.

"All right, team, let's talk about what this new role means for you and how you handle life outside these walls," he began, his voice carrying a reassuring tone. "What you're doing here is important work, but it's also unconventional-and it's not something you can just share with everyone." He paused, letting his words sink in. "First, let's discuss the story you'll tell your family and friends. Our work is covert, but we don't lie.

We're a government-supported organization focused on managing natural resources, ensuring sustainability, and promoting the positive impact of our efforts. Think of yourselves as part of an elite task force specializing in protecting and maintaining our environment. That's your truth."

Puck glanced around, catching a few nods.

Mr. Hardee continued, his tone warm but firm. "You can tell them your skills are being put to good use in specific roles, whether it's underwater conservation, resource management, wildlife protection, or technology. Explain that it's a position with certain confidential aspects and that, while you can't share everything, you're proud of the work you're doing to help make a difference."

"Honesty is key here, but you can keep some details vague."

He looked around the room, meeting each person's gaze. "If they ask where you're living, tell them this facility is equipped with full living quarters. It's convenient, it's part of the job, and you're welcome to stay here anytime. It's secure and provides the essentials you need-food, water, and a safe place to rest." A small smile touched his lips. "And yes, there's plenty of coffee on hand for the long days, and each of you will have access to basic amenities to make this place feel like home. But remember, you can come and go as you like. In the future, we can discuss this topic further, but for now, I think we should focus on building teamwork first."

Puck absorbed Mr. Hardee's words, his mind already racing with ideas on how to frame the conversation with his family. He was old enough to live independently and had been considering moving into a place of his own. This job was his opportunity to do so, and he felt both the weight and excitement of that decision.

Mr. Hardee concluded, "When you go home tonight, think carefully about how you present this. If you're approached with curiosity, stay confident in your answers. You're part of something bigger now, and that's something to be proud of."

Later, as Puck drove home with the darkened landscape rolling by, he rehearsed his conversation in his head. He would assure them it was a steady, full-time diving job and a step toward his future. He'd keep the details vague but honest, just as Mr. Hardee had said. Tomorrow, he'd be back for more training, ready to face the challenges ahead.

Puck stepped through the door into his parents' house, feeling the immediate warmth of home. The rich scent of his mom's cooking filled the air, a familiar comfort that made him realize how much he loved moments like these.

His parents welcomed him with open arms, his dad's usual hearty handshake turning into a tight hug. They guided him to the dinner table, where a spread of his favorite dishes awaited-each one a taste of home he hadn't realized he'd been craving.

As they sat around the table, he shared stories from his dives, carefully omitting details of the covert missions but letting his parents in on the beauty and excitement he experienced. He talked about clearing the underwater tunnel, the sprawling coral beds near the airplane, the group restoring the train, and the tranquility of the deep lake.

His parents listened intently-his dad nodding with interest and his mom's eyes lighting up with pride and curiosity. They continued to inquire about his work, but they were mainly intrigued by the adventures he had been involved in.

At one point, his dad gave him a firm pat on the shoulder. "Puck, we never doubted you for a minute! You've always fought for good and stayed true to your dreams. This world needs teams like yours to protect what we have. Seeing you follow your calling, it makes us proud beyond words."

His mom smiled warmly. "You've always dreamed about something bigger than yourself, Puck. It's wonderful to see it becoming a reality. We could not have hoped for a better path for you. Sure, we'll miss having you here every night, but you were made for this. It's your calling."

They moved to the living room, where his mom pulled out a book of memories they had made, filled with his childhood drawings-images of frogmen in diving suits exploring underwater worlds with schools of fish, sunken ships, and hidden caves. His dad chuckled, holding up one of the sketches.

"You were, what, seven? And already dreaming up gear for underwater exploration. We knew you'd go after big things."

Puck laughed, looking at the shaky lines he had once drawn with such care, each representing a piece of his young imagination. The drawings were filled with small details he had sketched to create his underwater adventure ideas that had only grown over the years alongside his best friends, Tad and Zane. His mom flipped through the pages, pointing out memories of the backyard experiments he used to run with Tad and the countless hours they had spent inventing stories of hidden treasure and unexplored ocean depths.

His gaze drifted to the corner of the room, where his old fish tank still stood. With its careful arrangement of stones, plants, and bright fish, it had once been a lesson in learning to balance his life. The hours he had spent cleaning, arranging, and feeding the fish had taught him patience, responsibility, and focus. It felt like a symbolic piece of his past-a quiet testament to the values he had nurtured before his dreams expanded to the depths of real oceans and rivers.

Book in hand, Puck sat down on the couch and closed his eyes.

"Thank you, God, for all these experiences," he exclaimed, feeling a connection between the past and the growing thought in his mind about Team TIDES.

Settled in the room where he used to read books full of underwater worlds, Puck realized just how much he owed to those early years: the support of his parents, the camaraderie with Tad and Zane, and the encouragement they had given each other to dream bigger. His parents had never discouraged his ambitions. Even when they seemed far-fetched. And now, sitting here, he could feel the fullness of that support, solid and unwavering.

As the night wore on, Puck made his way to the bedroom, pausing momentarily to take it all in. The familiar space held pieces of his childhood, reminders of who he was and the journey he had taken. He climbed into bed, pulling the covers over himself as a wave of contentment settled in. His mind drifted, carrying him back to the dream world he had often envisioned as a kid-the vast underwater landscapes lit by a soft glow. Only now, those scenes weren't just dreams; they were real places he had seen, explored, and learned to navigate.

Puck was back in the depths, surrounded by the quiet hum of the ocean. Fish swam by, moving in harmony, and the sunlight filtered down in beams, casting shifting patterns across the sand. He felt a deep sense of purpose, as though each dive and every mission was a step closer to something bigger, a current carrying him forward. The water enveloped him, the calm and rhythm of the ocean flowing around him like a silent promise, and he felt certain this was where he was meant to be.

The origins of his dreams, once as small as a mustard seed, had been nourished until they grew strong enough to support new adventures. Just one seed planted had yielded over a hundredfold. Puck's new team was part of that growth, not one person, not just one set of skills, but each member contributing to the whole.

That night, Puck dreamed of an octopus.

The next morning at dawn, the team began to assemble and prepare for their first official day. Puck and Tad decided to take the tunnel, eager to experience the thrill of the octopod transporting on a trial mission in sync mode. They headed to Matt's shop and found him already there, preparing an octopod.

"Great minds think alike!" Matt grinned, tapping the side of an octopod. "Figured you two might need a little room for your things at HQ."

Tad and Puck suited up and helped Matt prepare the first pod. They opened the second pod, set it to autopilot, and loaded it with a few belongings to help them settle in at the base. Once everything was secured, they launched into the tunnel, their heads-up displays syncing to the Vaultrium navigation. Other team members began joining the comms, their voices blending in warm greetings.

"Morning, everyone! It's a good day for training," came one cheerful voice. "I slept like a baby. What's that even mean, anyway? Ever been around a little one? They keep you up all night!"

The team shared a laugh, and the sense of camaraderie was tangible. Then, a familiar voice cut through the comms, clear and steady.

"Good morning, TIDES." Mr. Hardee's voice was unmistakable. "Training starts now. Dr. E and I have you up on hologram, and we've decided it's time to put your skills to the test."

Everyone perked up, their attention focused.

"Puck, Tad, your autopilot pod is taking a little detour. It's been rerouted, and you'll need to intercept it before it gets too far off course-or worse, lost. It's carrying some personal belongings for you two, so I imagine you'll want to handle this carefully. We're here to guide you. Let's show them what Team TIDES is made of!"

Puck and Tad exchanged a sudden glance, their nerves morphing into a determined focus. They had a plan, and their team was ready. Dr. E's voice chimed in next, full of energy. "All right, everyone. Engage your equipment in full sync, with hyper-realistic modes engaged. Let's get you locked in and ready. Puck, Tad, you're closest. Move in and echo your surroundings for the team!"

Puck and Tad maneuvered through the tunnels and caught up with the octopod in the lake at headquarters. They activated their sonar-equipped suits. Echoes bounced back to the team, transmitting real-time visuals to everyone's heads-up display, followed by optional routes to intercept in sync.

"Good work," Mr. Hardee's voice sounded again. "Now, a little twist for you. I've activated the pod's avoidance feature, so you'll have to get creative. Tad, Puck, I need you to stay close enough to engage your surroundings. Matt, Jordan, Derrick, and Austin, you're up."

Austin sped toward the lake, his hoverboard gliding just above the water's surface before shifting into high-speed aquatic mode. Jordan, on his ATV, plowed through shallow waters, which quickly transformed into aquatic mode as he hit a deeper section of the lake. Derrick's drones buzzed overhead, each equipped with directional sonic emitters.

"Let's bring that pod to a halt," Dr. E's voice came through with a grin. "Targeted sonic waves coming up."

Matt's octopod sped gracefully through the lake, pulsing out sonic waves that slowed the rogue pod just enough for a final play. Austin, Jordan, and Derrick locked sonic waves from opposite directions, steadying the octopod near the surface.

"All right, everyone, keep the pod in position," Mr. Hardee directed. "Zane, it's your turn."

Zane brought the plane down, smoothly shifting to hover mode just above the lake's surface. With precise timing, he activated the retractable grapple from the plane, expertly latching onto the pod and securing it. The team cheered through the comms as Zane lowered the pod onto the transport truck.
As the dust settled, a transport truck rolled into view with Dr. E and Mr. Hardee at the helm. Mr. Hardee's voice came through the comms, steady and clear. "Team, we're activating stealth mode. TIDES, align!"

With a single command, their gear synced, and each team member received directions through the fastest, stealthiest routes. The team moved as one, each individual focused, yet profoundly aware of the powerful purpose that bound them together. As they converged on the Vaultrium, their heads-up notifications activated, revealing projected stealth-mode locations alongside each member's true position. It was awe-inspiring technology woven into teamwork. Every element was precisely aligned with the design. Nothing was an accident. This was Team TIDES- moving in harmony like one unit, a single body composed of many members. Like the tentacles of an octopus, they worked seamlessly- camouflaging, protecting, and supporting each other.

"That's it," Puck said as they exited stealth mode, his voice filled with conviction. "We're meant to move as a team, each of us under authority, part of a whole unit. We're one body, with all abilities flowing together for a single purpose: for good."
The others responded one by one, their thoughts aligned as they echoed Puck's sentiment. Teamwork, Integrity, Dedication, Excellence, and Service- TIDES. Bound by these values, they understood their mission extended beyond themselves to a greater cause. The arms could never move without the head.

The Synchronium

Shortly after the alignment, they were all taken to the Synchronium, a state-of-the-art training facility designed to simulate real-world scenarios with advanced holographic and virtual reality technologies. This high-tech chamber would serve as their base for three intensive days of training.

Dr. E and Mr. Hardee began the briefing, emphasizing the urgency of their mission. "Mr. Becker and the environment can't wait any longer," Mr. Hardee said, his tone resolute. As the team gathered, they studied the layout of the RIPTIDE base through an interactive interface. Scans taken by Team TIDE's satellite provided detailed blueprints and environmental data, allowing the group to familiarize themselves with their target.

Inside the Synchronium, a holographic projection of the RIPTIDE base materialized-immersive and lifelike. The team virtually toured the base, running through various infiltration points and practicing scenarios tailored to their specific roles.

Tad and Puck focused on underwater entry, honing their skills with stealth maneuvers through a simulated underwater hatch. They practiced engaging RIPTIDE agents using nonlethal holographic measures such as taser darts, sticky nets, and decoy holograms. Every step required precision, teamwork, and adaptability.

Meanwhile, Zane mastered advanced flight techniques, rehearsing octopod recoveries and testing multiple approach angles with his plane. His nanobot flight suit allowed him to practice seamless transitions between piloting and midair extractions. Each simulation pushed him to refine his speed, accuracy, and coordination under pressure.

Derrick, Matt, Austin, and Jordan took charge of surface operations, conducting drills with boats, drones, and hoverboards. They ran diverse scenarios, preparing for enemy boats approaching from unexpected angles. They tested sonic disruptors and sticky catch nets, adjusting their tactics for various threat levels.

The training intensified as they incorporated dynamic challenges. In one sequence, Puck and Tad had to bypass a maze of holographic tripwires while neutralizing "guards." In another, Zane simulated aerial support, providing cover for Derrick's team as they deployed drones to disable enemy vessels. Every success and misstep was analyzed, ensuring the team adapted and improved with each attempt.

By the end of the second day, the Synchronium had become more than just a training space; it was their proving ground. The technology challenged them to the edge of their abilities, but it also brought them closer as a unit. They moved as one, their actions synchronized like a symphony.

On the final day, Dr. E addressed the team:

"You've all proven you have the skills, but remember, the key to this mission is trust and unity. Everything flows together, just like the design of creation itself. Work in sync, and you'll overcome whatever lies ahead. Remember, if one part of the body is injured, the whole body suffers. To have a functioning unit, you need all the components. A computer without a power source is not functional. Make sure you stay plugged into sync."

With their confidence and camaraderie strengthened, Team TIDES stood ready. Their mission to rescue Mr. Becker was no longer just a plan-it was certain.

Dr. E's voice came over the comms on the morning of the extraction, firm and filled with pride. "Today is the day. You've got this. We're designed to work together, to stand up to evil and be a voice for justice. There is no stronger love than love willing to lay itself down for another!" The line went quiet. Their purpose had never been clearer. Then Dr. E broke the silence, her words launching them into their next mission. "We will all meet in the Vaultrium for a mission briefing at the central holo-hub. See you there." With everyone gathered, Mr. Hardee and Dr. E pulled up a holographic map, pinpointing the structure off the coast-the RIPTIDE base.

"As you know from training in the Synchronium, Becker is here at their facility, a supposed 'research center' that is, in reality, one of RIPTIDE's illegal operations." His voice grew harder. "His suit has been transmitting data to us intermittently. Someone has been ensuring that the suit's core functions remain intact. They are exploiting resources and dumping waste that devastates marine life. If we don't take action, the ocean's oxygen levels in this zone will plummet rapidly."

Mr. Hardee's gaze swept the team. Focused, he addressed the plans again. "Puck and Tad, you'll take the tunnel to the open sea. Locate this access hatch and signal the team once you're ready. Engage full echo-sync stealth mode before entering the facility." He tapped a glowing spot on the hologram.

SONAR TOPOGRAPHY
MISSION OVERVIEW
SUBSEA
ACCESS HATCH
UNDERSEA
APPROACH ROUTE

"Zane," Mr. Hardee said, "you'll approach from the south. Wait for Puck and Tad's signal before moving in. Matt, Derrick, Jordan, and Austin, you'll pose as a commercial fishing crew, keeping watch while covertly aiding the team. Austin, contact the Coast Guard. This REDTIDE site is highly illegal, and EPA involvement will be crucial to our success."

Dr. E added, "Timing is critical. Yesterday's water tests show rapid oxygen depletion. By tonight, entire ecosystems could collapse. You've seen what TIDES can achieve in sync-this is our first real test as a team. Today, we show RIPTIDE what they're up against."

Mr. Hardee's voice steadied as he addressed them. "You've trained for this. Together, we'll stop them and bring Mr. Becker home. Your use-of-force suits are now active. Pull up your HUDs and review your options."

Their visors lit up, showcasing the range of nonlethal tools. Hardee gestured to the targets at the far wall. "Step to the line and prep for test fire."

Before they began, several Team TIDES workers stepped forward. "These tools are designed to neutralize without harm," Hardee explained. "Our volunteers are here to prove their safety."

Puck activated his watch and suited up first; the team followed his lead. Tranquilizer darts induced gentle drowsiness, sticky goo cannons immobilized, sonic pulses caused harmless disorientation, and ink blots cloaked the volunteers in harmless obscurity.

Hardee turned back to the team. "Painless but effective. The Synchronium was holographic training-this is the real thing. Now, monitor the patient."

Their HUDs displayed real-time data: target heart rate, blood pressure, oxygen saturation, and a countdown to recovery from the effects. Everything worked seamlessly, ultra-quiet, effective, and humane. Each incapacitated target's status was carefully monitored, ensuring their stability and health remained intact. Smiling, the volunteers gave thumbs-ups as the effects wore off.

Hardee nodded, satisfied. "This system provides full oversight. You'll be notified immediately of any medical needs a subject may have. If there's any sign of distress, we coordinate swift transport for treatment. Every individual you engage who has issues will receive top-tier medical care-and," he added with a hint of a smile, "free counseling from us."

The team exchanged determined nods, their resolve evident in their expressions. Hardee's sharp gaze swept across them. "Any final questions?"

Silence filled the room as anticipation thickened the air. Each member felt the gravity of the moment, and their focus sharpened. Team TIDES was ready to act.

With everyone geared up and prepared, Zane took the lead, transporting the boat crew to the commercial fishing vessel. He ensured every piece of mission gear was securely loaded before returning for the final briefing. Meanwhile, Puck and Tad entered the transport tunnels, syncing seamlessly with the rest of the team. Their intercept timing was perfectly calibrated, aligning precisely with the boat crew's arrival.

VISUAL ENHANCEMENT ACTIVE
SMART-MATERIAL ANALYSIS
STRAND INTEGRITY 92%
ADHESION LEVEL 68%
THERMAL READOUT
36.7°C
SYSTEM STATUS
NOTES
TEAM TIDES - OPERATIONAL OPTICS v4.2.1
SUBJECT ID: VRTM-0712-VAL | ROLE: SCIENTIST
ENVIRONMENT: VAULTRIUM TRAINING CENTER
TIME: 14:37:26 ZULU
SUBJECT STABLE
VITAL SIGNS: NOMINAL
NEURO RESPONSE: NORMAL
COGNITIVE FUNCTION: OPTIMAL
MUSCLE TONE: RELAXED
THREAT LEVEL: NONE
VISUAL ENHANCEMENT ACTIVE
MODE: MEDICAL SPECTRUM
FOCUS: SUBJECT / BIO FEEDBACK
BIOSCAN: LIVE
RESOLUTION BOOST
MICRO-CONTRAST
DEPTH CLARITY
SUBSURFACE ANALYSIS
CARDIAC MONITOR
HEART RATE
72 BPM
RESPIRATORY MONITOR
14 RPM
OXYGENATION
98%
PERFUSION INDEX
PI 4.6
NEURO STATUS
CNS LOAD 20%
SONIC RESPONSE ANALYSIS
SONIC FIELD MAPPING
FREQUENCY RANGE
18 Hz - 2.4 kHz
PRESSURE VARIATION
ACOUSTIC HARMONICS
STABLE
THERMAL READOUT
36.7°C
SYSTEM STATUS
NOTES
SUBJECT EXPERIENCING CONTROLL
NON-LETHAL SONIC-DISORIENTATI
VITALS STABLE.
RECOVERY ON TRACK.
SCIENTIFIC PROTOCOL VERIFIED.
TEAM TIDES - OPERATIONAL OPTICS v4.2.1
SUBJECT ID: VRTM-0712-V2 | ROLE: SCIENTIST
ENVIRONMENT: VAULTRIUM TRAINING CENTER
TIME: 14:47:19 ZULU
SUBJECT STABLE
VITAL SIGNS: NOMINAL
NEURO RESPONSE: NORMAL
COGNITIVE FUNCTION: OPTIMAL
MUSCLE TONE: RELAXED
THREAT LEVEL: NONE
VISUAL OBSCURATION ACTIVE
MODE: NON-LETHAL OBSCURATION
FOCUS: SUBJECT / NAVIGATION DISRUPTIO
BIOSCAN: LIVE
VISIBILITY REDUCTION 82%
ORIENTATION DISRUPTION: STABLE
TARGET LOCATOR: ADAPTIVE
CARDIAC MONITOR
HEART RATE
68 BPM
HRV 62 ms
RESPIRATORY MONITOR
14 RPM
TIDAL VOLUME 640 mL
OXYGENATION
98%
PERFUSION INDEX
PI 4.8
NEURO STATUS
CNS LOAD 18%
SMART-PARTICULATE ANALYSIS
CLOUD DENSITY 82%
ADHESION LEVEL 61%
NAVIGATION DISRUPTION
68%
MODERATE
RECOVERY PROJECTION
04:37
SUBJECT RECOVERY ON TRACK
NOTES
SUBJECT REMAINS CALM
AND COOPERATIVE.
OBSCURATION SYSTEM
PERFORMING WITHIN
SAFE HUMANITARIAN

As the fishing vessel neared the RIPTIDE base, the team checked in on comms. Their voices were professional and calm, echoing confidence. Puck and Tad confirmed their arrival with impeccable timing, their tones steady and clear. Zane hovered to the south, his ETA just sixty seconds.

"Activating full H.R.A.M.," Puck announced. "Echo-Sync online."

In perfect synchrony, they released the hatch, slipping into full camouflage mode. Their suits rendered them nearly invisible against the darkened base interior.

Inside, Mr. Hardee and Dr. E uploaded Mr. Becker's biodata to the suit scanners, instantly locking onto his location within the base. As Puck and Tad approached his quarters, they spotted two guards stationed at the door.

"I have left; Tad, take right," Puck murmured over comms.

Both took their positions, firing tranquilizer darts in flawless sync. The guards crumpled silently, their vitals remaining stable. With the area clear, Puck and Tad opened the hatch and stepped inside to find Mr. Becker, alert but bound by a heavy chain. Dropping out of camo mode, they greeted Becker, who managed a grin despite his restraints.

"Good to see you two-and all geared up with the team already. Nice."

"Likewise," Dr. E's voice cut in through comms. "Puck, activating your laser cutter."

Puck aimed the tool from his arm mount, slicing cleanly through the chain. As Becker rubbed his wrists, Tad's sensor pinged a nearby hostile moving toward them. He slipped back into camo mode, positioning himself by the door.

A RIPTIDE agent stepped down the last stair, pausing as he spotted the downed guards. He barely had time to draw a taser before Tad fired another dart, dropping the agent where he stood.

Tad immediately noted an anomaly in the agent's vitals. "We've got a RIPTIDE agent in distress. He needs treatment, a condition unrelated to the stun."

SECURED

Zane, from the plane, dropped an octopod from the rear hatch. Austin, on his hoverboard, zoomed over to prep the agent for emergency evacuation. Derrick, Matt, Jordan, and Jones deployed drones for cover, protecting the team. Tad swiftly disarmed the agent, checking for any hidden threats. Zane, in his flight suit, and Austin secured the agent inside the octopod. The pod's onboard medical system activated, stabilizing him as it transported him to the docks, where a TIDES ambulance awaited.

Meanwhile, Hardee coordinated security clearance and the medical handoff, ensuring a smooth transition. With the agent secured, Tad and Puck turned to Becker, who shook off the remnants of his confinement.

"Good to see you both. It's not the healthy who need a doctor, but the sick. Good handoff," Becker said. "I picked up a lot while I was here- no physical harm, but they tried to mess with my mind. Didn't work." He smirked. "They talked more than they should've. Turns out they've been stealing tech and forcing a scientist to hack it." Becker glanced at Puck. "I need my suit back if we're going to recover both."

"We've got you covered," Puck replied, handing him a nano watch. "Dr. E's latest gift."

Becker's eyes lit up. "She finally got it done! This changes everything." He suited up, syncing with the team as his HUD displayed their shared mission map. Scans pinpointed his original suit on the upper level of the base.

"Where my suit is, the scientist is likely close by," Becker said with a smirk. "That suit was how Dr. E and Hardee tracked me- RIPTIDE never figured that out."

"These suits are cutting-edge. Dr. E has built in every feature we could ask for, and then some-she can remotely load upgrades from the Forge. I tested the first prototype just before my capture, and I can't wait to see what this baby can do!"

Dr. E joked, "Choppa-choppa, get to doing! The clock's ticking!"

Dr. E confirmed the scientist's location from the satellite. "The hatch is eighty feet up, accessible from an exterior port door off the helipad," she informed them.

"Sounds like it's time to test the RGM mode," Becker replied.

The diagram immediately appeared on the HUD, with Dr. E confirming, "We have multiple climbing modes based on climbing frogs. This one, the 'Rainforest Gripper Mode,' mimics the red-eyed tree frog's suction grip, providing traction on wet, slippery surfaces."

The frogmen activated their suits' RGM mode. Their suits adapted quickly, adhesive pads forming on their gloves and feet.

"Woo-hoo!" Tad exclaimed. "Brand-new tech, first full day in the field!"

Outside, Zane pinged an approaching vessel. Jones launched a drone, capturing hull images and ID numbers. Moments later, Austin received confirmation from the Coast Guard, Shell Tech Inc., a RIPTIDE front company.

"Figures," Hardee muttered. "Their branding's as subtle as their tactics, a 'shell' company to hide their illegal activities."

Meanwhile, the boat crew braced as the RIPTIDE boat neared. Zane coordinated from the plane while Matt piloted drones toward the boat and armed the sticky nets. As the RIPTIDE crew approached, Derrick deployed focused sonic waves at the engine from his drone, disrupting the rhythm and slowing it down, while Matt released the nets, immobilizing the agents.

"Good catch," Jordan commented.

Within seconds, they had captured the crew and coordinated with law enforcement to secure the agents for processing.

Back outside, Puck leaped up the wall, with Tad and Becker following close behind. They skillfully navigated the slick surface as they advanced toward the lab hatch leading to the scientist's secure room, setting their sights on the last of their objectives.

The frogmen reached the hatch. Tad and Becker activated their stealth camo mode while Puck, disguised as a RIPTIDE agent, slipped through the door first. After he crossed the threshold, Tad and Becker moved in sync, positioning themselves to cover Puck's left and right flanks, quickly scanning the room. Only one RIPTIDE guard was present inside; Becker neutralized him with a quick dart. The vital scan remained stable. A scientist stood near his wife and daughter, their expressions tense but hopeful.

"We're here to help," Becker said as they disengaged their camo mode, revealing themselves. "You're safe now; the authorities are en route."

Puck looked at the scientist. "And you are...?"

Before the scientist could answer, Mr. Hardee's voice came over the comms.

"That's Dr. Zayler," Dr. E announced, "one of RIPTIDE's top former inventors."

Mr. Hardee added, "We met him years ago on a mission when he required immediate medical help. After a Team TIDES rescue, Dr. Zayler left RIPTIDE for good, and he's been a crucial ally ever since."

Becker shook Dr. Zayler's hand. "Good to see you again, Doc." Then, looking down at the young girl, he added, "Luna, right? You must be about fourteen now."

Luna nodded. "Yes! I just had my birthday this weekend. But, Mr. Becker, please, if you don't stop RIPTIDE, they'll destroy everything here!"

Dr. Zayler gestured toward a nearby terminal. "There's an access point over there. If you can hack in, you might be able to trigger a shutdown. But hurry, time's running out. Red Tide is already forming. We need to reverse the process and oxygenate the water quickly. We need to move fast-there are other RIPTIDE agents in the..."

02

Before he could finish, a loud, metallic clang echoed above them. Tad instinctively raised his weapon as Becker stepped protectively in front of Dr. Zayler's family. The top hatch creaked, and just as Puck turned to investigate, a side door near the helipad burst open, releasing a hiss of compressed air. Two figures emerged.

The first man strode forward confidently, his black suit gleaming under the fluorescent lights. A large circle glowed menacingly on his chest, and strange gloves hummed on his hands. The second figure was an enormous, robotic-looking man whose armor gleamed with patches of exposed metal. Red lights glowed like fiery eyes behind his face mask.

Dr. E's voice crackled urgently in their ears. "Team TIDES, those are RIPTIDE's elite enforcers-code names Eclipse and Ironshade. Be careful; they're equipped with some serious tech. One wrong move, and it's lights out!"

Mr. Hardee added gravely, "Expect the unexpected and work as a team. Stay focused, and watch each other's backs."

Eclipse sneered, his voice dripping with mockery. "Well, well. Team TIDES, come to play hero. How predictable."

Ironshade didn't speak, but the faint whir of servos and his imposing stance were enough to send a clear message: brute force.

"Divide and conquer," Becker said through their comms. "Tad, take Eclipse. Puck, you're with me on Ironshade. Stay nimble!"

Eclipse launched the first attack, forming a round black hole of goo with his glove. It splattered across the floor, sizzling as it ate through the surface. Tad vaulted over a railing, narrowly avoiding the attack.

"Aw, that reeks! What is that, your cologne?" Tad quipped, dodging another shot of goo. "No wonder you're single, Eclipse. I'm pretty sure even OSHA would ban that stuff."

A glob of goo struck Becker's glove, and alarms triggered in his heads-up display.

"Suit malfunction detected. Nanobots dispatched," announced the display, but before panic could set in, the nanobots reformed a new glove within seconds.

"Now that's what I call rapid recycling!" Becker quipped. "Keep moving!"

"Yeah, but don't let it touch your hair," Tad joked, ducking as Eclipse shot another round of black goo. "I doubt the nanobots can regrow that!"

Ironshade lunged at Puck, swinging a fist that dented the steel beam behind him as Puck dodged. The vibrations rattled through the room, but Puck stayed calm and returned a sonic blast at Ironshade.

"Becker, this guy's suit reflects our sonic blasts!" Puck shouted. "What now?"

"Stick to the flow in sync. Stay on him, I'll try the ink cloud!"

As Puck darted left, Becker activated a smoke cloud emitter, filling the space with a dense black mist. But Ironshade's helmet glowed with an eerie infrared hue.

"He's got IR vision!" Puck called out, flipping over a console as Ironshade barreled toward him.

"Switching to Plan B," Becker replied, sprinting along the wall and firing a sticky goo net at Ironshade's legs. The netting slowed him, but the hulking man's sheer strength began tearing through the goo.

Meanwhile, Tad had Eclipse on the defensive. "You like goo? Try some of ours!" he shouted while taking a shot. Eclipse sidestepped, but Tad was already above him, launching a tranquilizer dart. It grazed Eclipse's arm, but the man snarled and retaliated with another ring of goo, forcing Tad to leap backward.

"You're quick," Eclipse growled, "but not quick enough!" He depressed the circular eclipse symbol on his chest. The lights blacked out, and the room vibrated as an energy pulse disrupted the agents' suits momentarily. Ironshade's armor seemed unaffected.

Becker's suit rebooted just in time. "ANV online. Tad, Puck- sync up. Amphibian Night Vision engaged! We've got one shot to take these guys down!" Their mask lenses employed night vision.

Puck nodded. "Ready when you are!"

Becker coordinated the attack. "On three: Tad, go high. Puck, flank Ironshade. I'll draw their attention. One . . . two . . . three!"

Becker charged at Eclipse, zigzagging to avoid the goo while launching sonic pulses to distract him. Tad vaulted off a beam, landing squarely on Eclipse's back and injecting a tranquilizer directly into his arm.

Ironshade roared, swinging wildly as Puck darted behind him. Using his suit's agility in RGM mode, Puck scaled the wall and leaped onto Ironshade's back. He fired a dart at the top part of Ironshade's shoulder, just between the armor's protective plating.

The tranquilizer took effect. Eclipse collapsed first; his defeat was certain. Ironshade staggered, his movements slowing until he fell to one knee, then crumpled forward. Both subjects' vitals were displayed as normal.

"Targets neutralized," Becker said, panting. "Great work, team."

Puck grinned, wiping his forehead. "Let's hope RIPTIDE doesn't have a round two planned."

"Agreed," Tad added, shaking his head. "I think our suits deserve a medal. What we just went through was anything but normal."

Becker laughed. "Yeah, I'm glad their vitals are fine. If this is normal for RIPTIDE, I'm rethinking our hazard pay."

Dr. Zayler approached cautiously, glancing at the RIPTIDE agents. "That was... impressive. The synchronization of your moves, the adaptability of your suits- it's far beyond what I've seen before." He gestured to the downed Eclipse. "And his tech... It's something new, even for RIPTIDE. We'll need to study it."

"Later," Becker replied, rolling his shoulders. "For now, we've got a base to shut down."

Puck nodded, his expression serious. "Let's move. Every second counts."

The team regrouped, each taking their positions to finish the mission. As they approached the terminal, Dr. Zayler murmured, "You may have taken out their top agents, but you'll need to be ready for what comes next. They won't stop."

"We won't either," Puck said firmly, activating his drone.

Puck's mini drone launched off his forearm and zipped to the control panel. Dr. E guided Puck from her remote station, inputting deconstruction and reset commands while Mr. Hardee initiated a facility-wide environmental recalibration.

"Let's reverse what damage we can by upgrading their system and making this base a source of restoration, not pollution," Dr. E said.

Meanwhile, outside the facility, Jones and Jordan prepared specialized drones, coordinating to conduct a final security sweep. Austin darted to the station's core output on his hoverboard, scanning environmental readings and spraying a bio-restorative agent to neutralize hazardous levels. The mist settled, transforming the area into a healthier zone as friendly bacteria spread and supported a cleaner ecosystem.

Once the reset was underway, Puck, Tad, and Becker guided Dr. Zayler and his family to the helipad. Zane swooped in, expertly maneuvering the aircraft as he picked them up. The team completed the final sweeps of the base, securing any data or remnants to hand over to the authorities.

Within minutes, EPA and Coast Guard officials arrived to find the facility systematically secured, thoroughly documented, and primed for their investigation. After coordinating with the authorities, the team reconvened. Mr. Hardee's voice came over their comms, signaling their mission's final directive.

TEAM TIDES

The Light in the Darkness

"All right, team-TIDES, align."

In unison, the team confirmed the order. Adrenaline still pumped from the mission as each member moved with purpose and unity, converging on the Vaultrium-Team TIDES' nerve center. Their first successful mission together felt monumental, and they made their entrances count. Octopods arrived with mechanical precision, while Zane, still in his flight suit, remotely piloted the plane, slicing through the sky in celebration. Puck, Tad, and Becker burst from the transport tunnels, each sticking a perfect landing in Frogman Bay.

Inside the Vaultrium, Mr. Hardee addressed them, his voice deep with gratitude. "Job well done, Team TIDES. This mission proved your courage, skill, and devotion to the principles we live by. The light shines a ray of hope because of each of you-each step taken to safeguard what matters."

Dr. Zayler stepped forward, emotion in his eyes. "Thank you for bringing me back to the light again. RIPTIDE... they're growing faster than we anticipated. Their goals are insidious-twisting technology meant for good into a weapon of control and destruction. They're taking what was meant to nurture and using it to devour."

He glanced at his daughter, Luna, standing resolute beside him. "They are the polar opposite of everything we believe in. It's night and day-darkness and light. We named her Luna because, like the moon, God gives us light even in the darkest night.

"When I was lost in RIPTIDE's lies, He provided a lighthouse, guiding me out of that darkness. Without it, I wouldn't have seen her grow up. He brought His light to me-just like when He sent His light to us."

"It gave me a second chance to undo the harm I'd once been part of spreading. RIPTIDE isn't just an enemy; it's a sickness, a parasite leeching away what's good and true in this world." Zayler paused, lifting his gaze. "Like the stars and the moon that light the night's sky, showing people that God's light is a hope in the darkness to guide us back to Him. The moon may only reflect the sun, but it reminds us that hope never dies. Even in the darkness, it guides the tides. It's like the prodigal son who was lost but finally opened his eyes and followed the path home to the Father."

The room was silent for a moment before Mr. Hardee and Dr. E approached Dr. Zayler.

"Dr. Zayler, tell us more."

"I need to tell you-they know. RIPTIDE's caught wind of your latest project-the symbiotic prototype you've been developing at the warehouse. They had it at their facility for a time, hoping to force me to reverse-engineer it for their own twisted purposes. I told them it was way beyond my skill, which was true enough. But I knew whose handiwork I was seeing-Dr. E, your brilliance was woven all through its defenses."

Dr. E's eyes narrowed. "They tried to make you turn it against us?"

"Yes," Zayler nodded. "They asked me to make it parasitic instead of symbiotic-and to hack Becker's suit too. I stalled, knowing I could keep the suit's core features intact. They wanted the suit, the prototype, and you. I love these new suits you're all wearing, nano-tech-adaptive, right? Anyway, I knew Team TIDES would return. So here we are, together, ready to outshine the shadows."

Becker gripped Zayler's shoulder. "You kept the suit safe, and you kept yourselves safe. That was the best chance you could've given us."

TIDES
Research and
Environmental
Stewardship
Institute
WELCOME

Dr. Zayler took a deep breath, nodding toward Luna. "And now, I see that light isn't just here in the Vaultrium- it's alive in each of you. You have what it takes to beat RIPTIDE, to show them that everything should be founded on God's truth."

Puck, a resolute look on his face, spoke up. "It's all coming together. In the face of our struggle against these forces, I'm starting to see how each piece fits. The octopus- that's us, the unit working together. The moon... It's the light in the darkness. It's not the source of light itself but a reflection of truth. Just as the moon guides the tides, we're here to work as one body, to guide others to the light, and to push back when RIPTIDE's waves crash against us.

"With God's truth and light on our side, we are prepared to stand firm. No matter where you are in the world, everyone can see one or more sources of light each day. The sun, the moon, and the stars shine on us all. We aren't the light-we reflect it and point the way. Light cuts through the darkness, and we will let the light shine to illuminate the path."

Dr. Zayler glanced at Puck, nodding in approval as Puck continued. "People need to dream big and have their own origin stories, and this-this is our origin story. We'll fight for what's right, protect those who need it, and pray for those who haven't yet stepped into the light to find their way back to the Father through the Son- just like you did, Dr. Zayler. This is something we must hand down to those who come after us."

Dr. E stepped forward, an encouraging smile on her face. "Puck, you're exactly right. Speaking of others coming into the light, I've got an update for you all. The RIPTIDE agent who needed medical assistance... he's awake, stable, and asking to speak with you. He knows you all rendered aid."

Puck's eyes lit up with anticipation. "We'll be there," he said, his voice steady with purpose.

"Count me in, too!" they all chimed in as the rest of the team murmured their agreement.

Mr. Hardee chuckled. "Looks like we'll have a full house. Don't worry, we'll make room. But for now, Dr. E has been working on something special that she's eager to show you. After that, clean up for a hot meal."

Dr. E clapped her hands, motioning to the large holographic display. "Chopa-chopa, gather around! I know each one of you has your own unique gifts, so we've created customized living quarters for each of you based on your interests and talents. A crew of drones, robots, and workers completed it overnight." She pressed a button, and the hologram screen came alive with detailed layouts-each scene met with excited gasps and exclamations from the team.

"Puck, Tad," she began, "I thought you two might appreciate an underwater superbase. You'll have your separate quarters and a spacious common room with porthole windows offering underwater views, and we've incorporated elements that reflect your shared memories from Starlight Cove. There's even a living pool with lily pads to give you a slice of home and remind you of your dreams."

Puck and Tad exchanged wide-eyed looks, trying to take it all in.

"This is amazing, Dr. E," Tad whispered, barely able to contain his excitement.

"Zane," Dr. E continued, "your apartment is right above theirs with a special air-powered transport tunnel, like those tubes at the bank that shoot things back and forth. Just think of it as your portal to the skies."

Zane grinned, shaking his head in awe. "The only thing missing is a parachute station," he joked, earning a round of laughter.

"Derrick," Dr. E went on, "you're in the communications tower, fully equipped to handle everything from intelligence gathering to mission planning. And yes, the entire tower is interconnected with the other rooms for seamless access."

"Sweet," Derrick replied, looking impressed. "I've always wanted a room with a view."

"Austin, you'll have an eco-friendly suite on the lake's surface, with glass walls for a clear view of the water. It even has a blackout mode for privacy, and, of course, it's connected to the main group tunnel."

Jordan's eyes lit up as Dr. E continued. "And for you, we've designed a futuristic, heavy-duty vehicle that docks right onto the main tunnel. You'll have the best of both worlds: mobility and access to the entire base."

Dr. E turned to Matt, her smile widening. "You have your very own place on the lake's edge, with a tunnel that connects back to your original shop, allowing you to travel back and forth in minutes by octopod.

"As for you, Jones," she added with a knowing grin, "we built you a metalworks loft right above the main engineering bay, nestled at the forest's edge. It's part workshop, part retreat-every tool you could want, a custom-built forge, and reinforced worktables to handle whatever you dream up. The walls are lined with schematics and prototype stations. And your sleeping quarters? A perfect blend of industrial and comfort. Since we know you like camping and cooking, we added a wraparound deck with a forest view and a fully stocked kitchen-just in case you feel like grilling under the stars."

As Dr. E showcased each setup, the team's reactions were off the scale. Every room was interconnected through an elaborate system of tunnels, with different access points, some above ground with air-powered transport tubes, others underwater for their frogman entrances. Each space was thoughtfully tailored to their strengths, making it the ultimate headquarters.

Finally, Mr. Hardee cleared his throat. "All right, team, as Dr. E says, 'Chopa-chopa! Get cleaned up, eat up, and then check out your quarters.' You can relax in the common room where all the rooms connect or settle into your own space for the night."

As the team began to disperse, the sound of hurried footsteps echoed down the hall. A man burst into the room, slightly out of breath and clutching a laptop. His face was flushed with urgency and excitement.

"Dr. E! Wait!" he called out, his voice cutting through the low hum of conversation.

Everyone turned toward him. Dr. E straightened, immediately alert.

"What is it, James?" she asked, recognizing the engineer under her command.

"I have it!" James exclaimed, holding up the laptop. "We figured out more of the artifacts' significance in this whole mystery!"

Dr. E moved quickly toward him, taking the laptop and scanning its contents. Her eyes flickered with recognition, then intrigue, as she scrolled through the data. After a moment, she nodded, her expression shifting to one of deep thought.

"Interesting. Very interesting," she murmured before closing the laptop and turning to the team. "Everyone, listen up. This is important."

The team focused on Dr. E with anticipation. She clasped her hands behind her back, her voice steady and commanding as she began to speak.

"The first artifact, the bottle in the attic, was more than just an antique. It served as a lens, much like glasses. It allowed us to see the path ahead with clarity, revealing a map hidden within its intricate carvings. This lens taught us that perspective matters-without the ability to see clearly, the journey ahead is shrouded in confusion."

She clicked a remote, and the hologram above the table displayed the moonlit artifact. Its intricate design shimmered as it rotated slowly.

"Next came the Moonlight Artifact, recovered from the lake. Derrick and Puck retrieved this piece, which held a powerful message. It symbolized the importance of staying on the narrow path illuminated by truth. In darkness, the path forward becomes treacherous, but with light as your guide, you can navigate the unknown. This artifact represents a light we carry with us, reminding us to seek clarity and stay steadfast."

MOONLIGHT ARTIFACT ANALYSIS
FULL SPECTRUM SCAN
GEOMETRIC PATTERNS
POSSIBLE INTERFACE POINTS
ENERGETIC SIGNATURE STABLE
PURPOSE UNKNOWN

The hologram shimmered, shifting to an image of the airplane artifact. Dr. E gestured toward it, her voice steady with intrigue.

"The artifact hidden within the airplane is particularly fascinating. It showcases principles of flight engineering in a way that speaks to intentional design. Above the octopus emblem, two cross-sections of an airplane wing are displayed, illustrating the concept of the 'angle of attack.'"

She paused for emphasis, clicking to magnify the holographic display.

"The angle of attack," she explained, "is the angle between the relative wind and the chord line of the wing. It's critical for generating lift. Too steep an angle, and you experience a stall, losing the ability to fly. Too shallow, and it cannot generate enough lift to rise. The artifact serves as more than a technical piece; it's a profound reminder of how approach matters in everything."

Austin tilted his head, intrigued. "But what about those unseen forces-air molecules-how do they know what to do?"

Dr. E smiled, her tone purposeful.

"Exactly, Austin. The unseen forces, the precise physics of flight, are part of a design so intricate that it works perfectly whenever the approach is correct. It's a lesson for all of us. Just as unseen air molecules lift a wing, unseen principles-faith, preparation, purpose-propel us to greater heights. But it all begins with recognizing and trusting in that design."

With a click, the hologram transitioned to an image of the train artifact.

"And now, we come to the train," Dr. E continued.

The hologram displayed the mechanical octopus, its arms intricately surrounded by three distinct features: a gear, a compass, and a clock.

"This," she said, gesturing toward the projection, "is the mechanical gear octopus-a marvel of craftsmanship. The gear cradles a compass, which rests atop a clock. It represents precision, direction, and timing-all necessary for purpose-driven work."

Her expression grew thoughtful.

"The original team designed the train to transport timber, aiding in the construction of this town. It was built for strength and resilience, capable of carrying immense loads. But here's the critical part: without its tracks-its narrow, fixed path- it is powerless. A train's strength and potential mean nothing if it strays from the course designed for it. The lesson here is clear: we, too, must stay on track to fulfill the purpose for which we were created."

Dr. E's voice dropped slightly, adding weight to her next words. "The second element within the train was a bottle, carefully sealed and hidden in a concealed compartment. Its surface bore the etched image of a ship with sails unfurled- a clue, perhaps, to one of our next destinations. But the true revelation was the third element inside the bottle."

She held up a projection of its contents: a weathered map and a riddle inscribed in elegant, flowing script:

"The light of space stands tall in its place,
Rooted on earth, below the hands that trace,
The flow of time to guide the vessel,
That bears the weight of what truly matters.
Take with you what you have discovered,
For only together will the truth be uncovered."

The room fell silent as the team digested the cryptic lines.

Dr. E turned to the group. "Thoughts?"

Puck was the first to speak. "The light of space standing tall-that has to be a lighthouse, right? But which one? There are several in the area."

Matt leaned forward, his face alight with recognition. "My grandfather used to tell stories about the old Light Keepers," he said. "They didn't just tend the lighthouses-they were also responsible for keeping the town's clock and managing the historical library. He used to say they were protectors of more than just light-they safeguarded knowledge and the history of time."

Mr. Hardee nodded thoughtfully. "The lighthouse and clock are both 'rooted on earth,' just like the riddle says. And the hands of the clock trace time. If these Keepers were the guardians Matt's grandfather spoke of, they might have left behind records-or clues-about how to proceed. A trip to the Keepers' Library seems like our next logical step."

Dr. E's eyes narrowed as she considered their words. "It makes sense. If the Light Keepers were connected to the artifacts somehow, the library might hold the key to unlocking this riddle."

Puck's expression brightened as a thought struck him. "And what about the last part of the riddle? 'Take with you what you have discovered, for only together will the truth be uncovered.' I think it means we're going to need to bring the artifacts with us. They're not just clues-they're part of the mechanism, like keys to unlocking whatever the Keepers left behind."

Matt nodded, his voice steady with conviction. "If the legends about the Keepers are true, their work was deeply rooted. It wasn't just about maintaining physical structures-it was about preserving something far greater: fellowship, truth, and purpose-things that matter most."

Mr. Hardee leaned forward, his expression thoughtful yet firm. "We need to narrow down which lighthouse and clock the riddle is pointing to. But if these artifacts are keys, as Puck suggests, then we're not just solving a puzzle; we're continuing the work of the Keepers. Staying on the right path, just as they did, will be critical to uncovering the next step."

Dr. E's fingers flew across her keyboard as the others spoke. Suddenly, her expression shifted, and she glanced up with a hint of excitement. "I think I've found something," she said, her voice calm but tinged with urgency. "There's a library called the Harbor Light Archives. According to this historical brief, it dates back to the mid-1800s. It was originally established by a group known as the Coastal Preservation Society. They were also caretakers of lighthouses and stewards of history, preserving the area's most vital historical accounts and values."

"That's got to be it," Matt said, leaning closer to the screen as Dr. E turned it toward them. "Harbor Light Archives? That's practically screaming Keeper's Library!"

Dr. E closed her laptop with a decisive click. "All right, team. We've got a direction. The Harbor Light Archives will be our starting point. But we need to proceed carefully; if the artifacts truly act as keys, then we'll need to protect them at all costs. There's no telling what's coming next."

N
11
12
1
10
2
W
E
8
4
7
5
S

The team dispersed, retreating to their rooms to get ready for dinner. The air buzzed with excitement as they settled in for their meal, laughing and recounting the day's events. After dinner, they explored their rooms more thoroughly, marveling at the thoughtful details in each setup. Every feature was carefully designed to sustain life while offering personal touches-a place to live, crafted with each of them in mind.

Puck and Tad entered their underwater apartments-a world they had only dreamed of as kids. Through the large, round glass windows, they watched fish glide by while bubbles drifted to the surface, casting soft ripples of light into their space. It felt like they were back in Starlight Cove, surrounded by the glow of the stars reflecting off the water.

Puck tapped the comms device, calling Zane down to the "Cove," as they had nicknamed it. Zane appeared on the display, grinning as he greeted them.

"This is awesome! I'm calling my place 'Starlight Overwatch.' You have to see it next!"

Zane tubed in and joined them in the Cove as they reflected on their journey. They laughed, shared memories, and spoke about the power of the light that shone through their lives and work.

"Air meets water here, just like our dreams meet reality," Zane said thoughtfully. "It's not just teamwork- it's family. It's a fellowship."

Soon, the entire team joined in on sync mode from their private rooms, reflecting on the mission ahead. Their conversation grew serious as they discussed plans to meet the recovering RIPTIDE agent and uncover the mystery behind the remaining artifacts. They agreed to sleep on it, each knowing the road ahead would be filled with challenges.

Before signing off, they tossed out ideas for team nicknames, laughing and teasing each other with wild suggestions. Tad was completely against being called "Tadpole." After several rounds of playful banter, they finally said goodnight, each logging off and settling into the peace of their private quarters.

Puck lingered a moment longer, looking out through the glass porthole as bubbles rose slowly before him, drifting upward like tiny silver balloons. The clear lake waters around him were calm, illuminated by the pale glow of the moon filtering through the surface above. He remembered when his only glimpse into this world had been through rain-speckled windows and the vibrant pages of adventure books. Back then, a stormy day was enough to turn his living room into an underwater observation deck, his windowpanes into imaginary portholes, and his heart into a compass pointing toward the sea.

Tonight, he was no longer the boy peering into those imaginary realms but a frogman in his underwater sanctuary. Vibrant fish no longer just woven into the patterns of his childhood rug, now darted through the lake's depths, occasionally brushing by the porthole, curious yet elusive. A familiar shape stirred outside-this time, not a giant turtle with wise eyes but a frog perched on a rock by the glass, its small, glistening eyes gazing in as if in silent encouragement. It was a gentle reminder of the journey from the dreams of a boy to the reality of a man, diving deep into life's mysteries.

He connected with Tad one last time in private sync mode. Memories of their conversations echoed in his mind, as clear and persistent as the quiet hum of his SCUBA equipment.

"Have you ever seen the 'bubble-up men' on TV?" Puck had asked Tad with childlike awe years ago.

Tad chuckled across the line. "Bubble-up men? What do you mean?"

"They dive deep into the ocean," Puck explained. "They wear fins, masks, and big air tanks. When they breathe, bubbles float to the surface like tiny silver balloons!"

Tad laughed as they both vividly recalled the memory from long ago. "Ah, frogmen-or SCUBA divers. They explore the underwater world."

"A frogman," Puck whispered, smiling as he spoke aloud. "That's what I wanted to be."

Without any further discussion on the subject, Puck and Tad exchanged their good nights, each quietly thanking God for the journey that had brought them here. Tonight was the culmination of everything: the dreams they had chased together, the fears they had faced, and the bond forged through shared wonder.

As Puck closed his eyes, the soft flicker of moonlight danced across his porthole, like a gentle reminder of the old adventure books and TV channels that had once fed his curiosity. He could almost see his childhood self reflected in the glass-the boy with wide eyes and endless questions who had longed for this very life. The once-fanciful porthole he had stared through from the safety of his home was now a reality surrounding him. With every mission, he answered the call that had tugged at him all those years ago, unlocking secrets hidden deep within the lakes, rivers, and seas. Tomorrow, with the sun's first light breaking over the lake, he would rise once again to join Team TIDES. They would set out not just to explore but to preserve the wonders he had once imagined. The lake whispered around him, as if promising more mysteries to be unraveled and deeper places to explore. In this quiet underwater world, Puck drifted to sleep, the lake gently cradling him like the pages of his childhood books, closing one chapter, only to open another. There was so much more to discover when the sun rose. As the waters settled into silence, he knew this was just the beginning of an adventure beyond his wildest dreams.

Personal Message From Joel

I truly hope you experienced a faith-filled adventure as you read this book. Now, what's next? Continue to grow in your faith and walk with the Lord. Share your faith boldly-if you know the Truth, what better gift can you give than pointing others to the Savior who rescues us from a life separated from Him? Don't worry about hurting anyone's feelings or how your words might be received. Tell your story: why you have faith, what you've observed, and what sparked your trust in Christ. That is the essence of witnessing.

Stay true to God's Word, remain vigilant against false teachings, and measure every idea against Scripture. Pray for wisdom and guidance so that the Truth shines forth. The Bible warns us that false gospels exist-disguised as angels of light or as wolves in sheep's clothing-so hold fast to the core values of Scripture and the principles of salvation without compromise.

Each one of us has a unique role in the Body of Christ, sharing the one gospel message-the good news of Christ's sacrifice, death, and resurrection-that brings salvation. These books are built on real stories of faith in action, celebrating the wonder of God's handiwork. My hope is that this content leads even one person into a relationship with Christ, making every hour of writing worthwhile.

I pray that believers will use this material to reach non-Christians so that the Truth may be known. If you found inspiration in this book, the mentor's guide, or the standalone story, please take a few minutes to share your experience in a review.

Thank you for joining me on this quest!

In Christ,

Joel Chanaca

About the Author

Joel Chanaca is a four-time Global Book Awards–winning author, recognized for his contributions to Humor and Heart and Hunter, the English Setter. This book, "Origins," won the gold medal, and Patches the Cat is a Thief: The 2025 Edition won the bronze medal in 2025! A dedicated game warden with over twenty-five years of law enforcement experience, Joel has spent his career in public safety and wildlife law enforcement.

From an early age, Joel embraced adventure-camping, fishing, canoeing, and scuba diving-experiences that would later inspire his storytelling. His deep appreciation for nature has only grown through his work in natural resource protection, reinforcing his belief in the beauty and complexity of God's creation.

"The elements of design are all around us. If we take the time to pause and look, we can see how God has made a place for us. More than just the wonders of the earth, His plan extends beyond the physical world. Through Christ, we are offered the ultimate gift of salvation-a sacrifice made so that He could prepare a place for us beyond what we can see."

Your Honest Review Makes a Difference

"I hope Frogman Puck Origins: The Rising Tides brings adventure, wholesome values, teamwork, friendship, and Godly lessons into your life. If you enjoyed this book, please take a few minutes to leave an honest review. Your feedback makes a difference!"

Thank you, Joel

Thank You for Joining the Adventure

If you've made it this far, thank you for spending time with Puck and Team TIDES.

I hope this story reminded you of the wonder of discovery, the excitement of adventure, and the courage to answer life's greatest callings.

This is only the beginning.

There are more mysteries to uncover, more adventures waiting beneath the surface, and a growing community of readers who believe every great adventure begins with a calling.

Stay Connected

Leave an Honest Review

Your review helps other readers discover Frogman Puck and supports future adventures.

[AMAZON QR CODE]

[BOOKBUB QR CODE]

[GOODREADS QR CODE]

Thank you for becoming part of Team TIDES.

Take a deep breath.

The water is calm.

The mystery is still waiting.

See you on the next adventure.

— Joel Chanaca

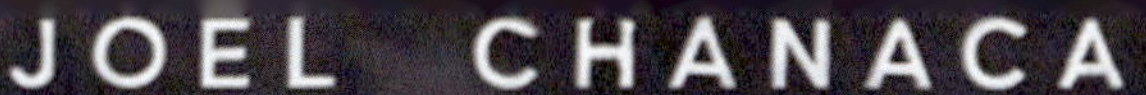

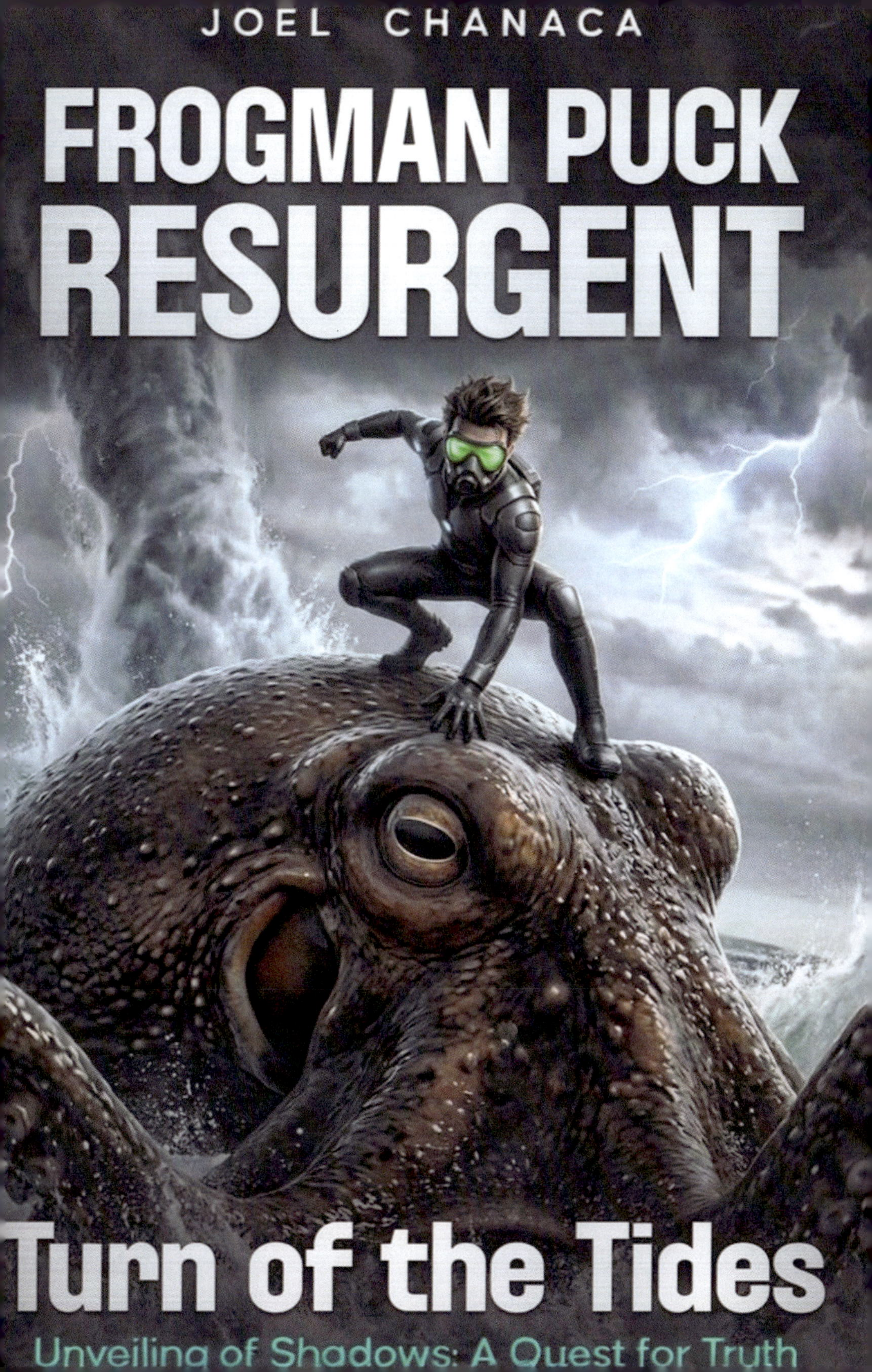
JOEL CHANACA
FROGMAN PUCK
RESURGENT
Turn of the Tides
Unveiling of Shadows: A Quest for Truth

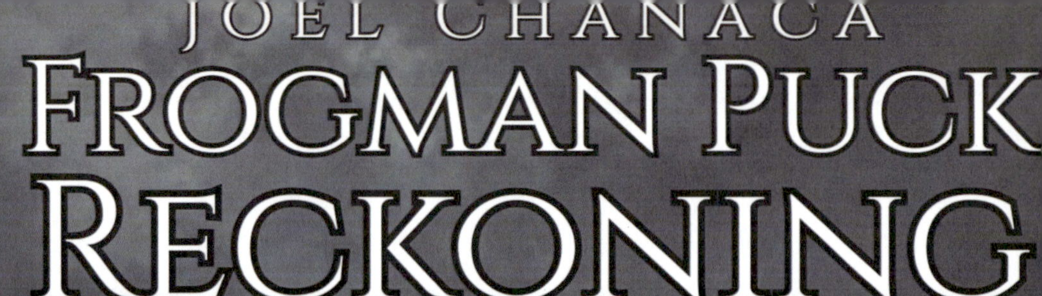

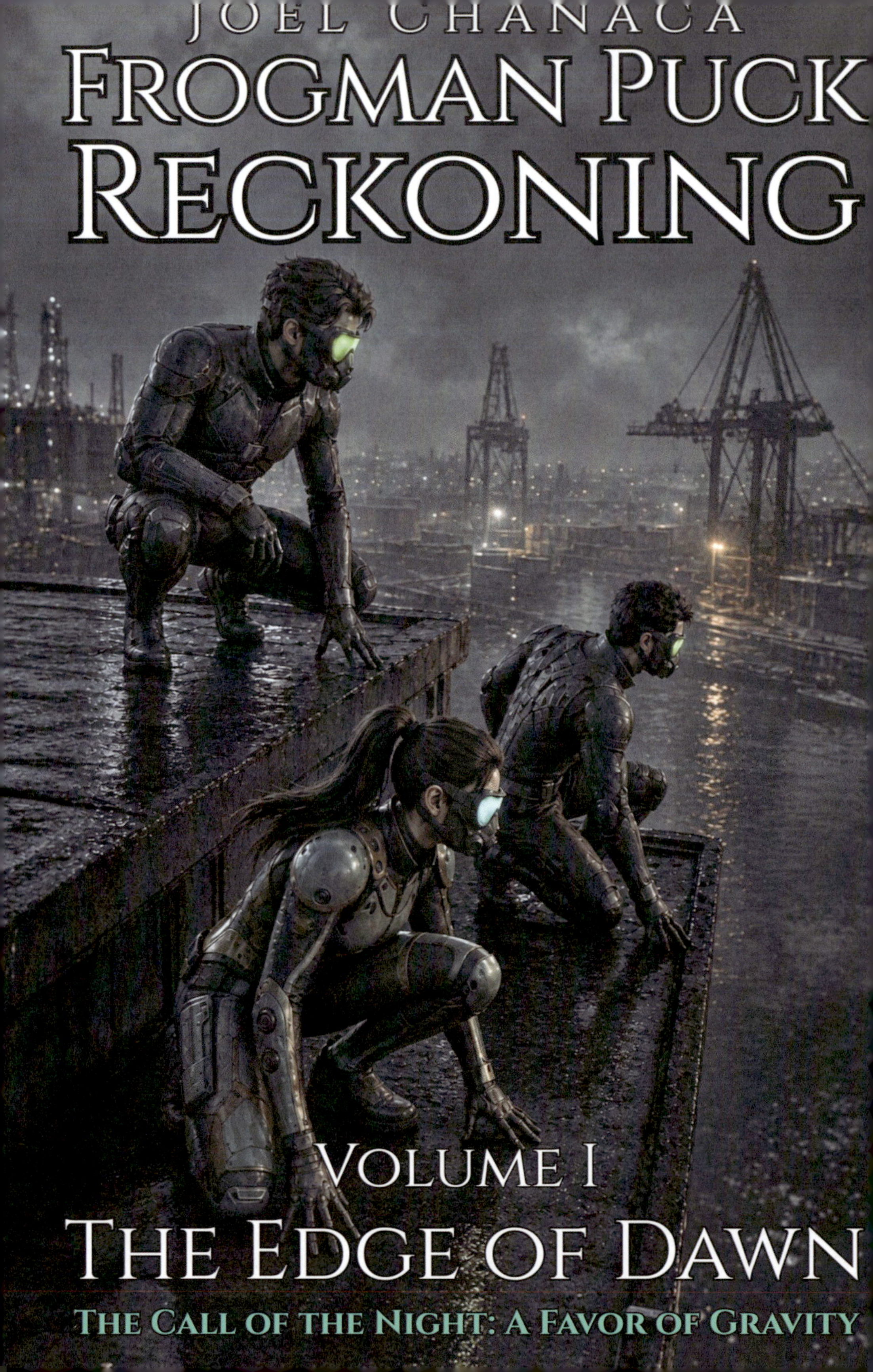
JOEL CHANACA
FROGMAN PUCK
RECKONING
VOLUME I
THE EDGE OF DAWN
THE CALL OF THE NIGHT: A FAVOR OF GRAVITY

JOEL CHANACA

FROGMAN PUCK RECKONING

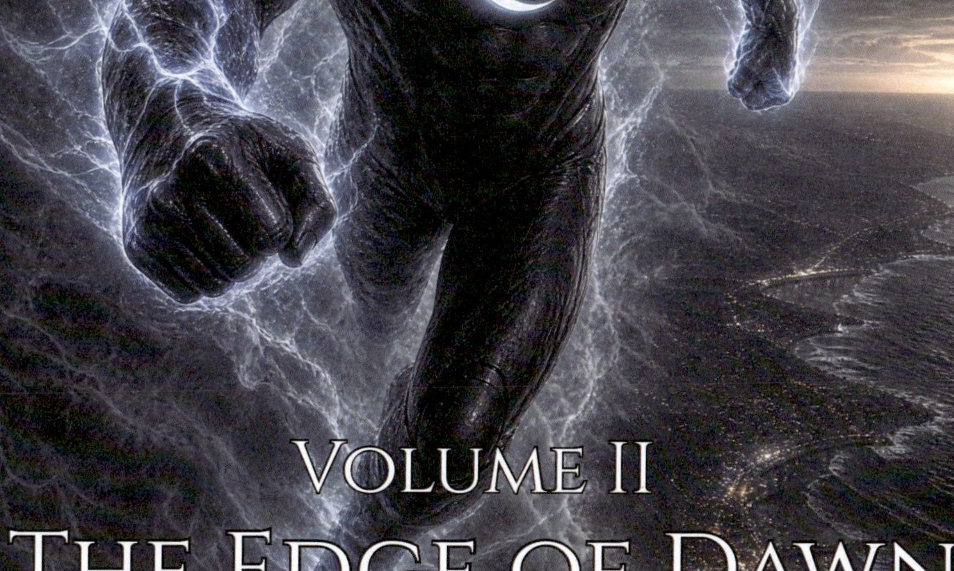

VOLUME II

THE EDGE OF DAWN

THE BEASTS OF SHADOW AND LEGEND: BENEATH THE BLACK CURRENT

JOEL CHANACA

FROGMAN PUCK RECKONING

VOLUMES I & II

The Edge of Dawr

Night of the Meridian: Horizon of Justice

www.ingramcontent.com/pod-product-compliance
Lightning Source LLC
Chambersburg PA
CBRC101355060826
49398CB00048B/132

9781963416275